25/01

A NEW WINDMILL BOOK OF FANTASY AND SCIENCE FICTION

INTO THE UNKNOWN

Edited by Steve Barlow and Steve Skidmore

Heinemann
New Windmills

Heinemann Educational Publishers
Halley Court, Jordan Hill, Oxford OX2 8EJ
A division of Reed Educational and Professional Publishing Ltd

OXFORD MELBOURNE AUCKLAND
JOHANNESBURG BLANTYRE GABORONE
IBADAN PORTSMOUTH (NH) USA CHICAGO

04 03 02 01
10 9 8 7 6 5 4 3 2 1

ISBN 0 435 12534 6

The publishers gratefully acknowledge the following for permission to reproduce copyright
material. Every effort has been made to trace copyright holders, but in some cases this has
proved impossible. The publishers would be happy to hear from any copyright holder that has
not been acknowledged.

'Feeding Time' by James Gunn © 1955 by Street & Smith Publications; renewed 1983 by James
E. Gunn; reprinted with permission of the author. 'To Serve Man' by Damon Knight, published
in 1950 by Galaxy Science Fiction; reprinted with permission of the author. 'Artificial
Intelligence' from *Sensational Cyber Stories* collected by Tony Bradman © Malorie Blackman
1998; reprinted with permission of A.M. Heath & Co Ltd. 'Surfer and the Dreamcastle' by Steve
Bowkett; reprinted with permission of the author. 'Into The Shop' by Ron Goulart © 1970
Mercury Press Inc.; first published in *The Magazine of Fantasy and Science Fiction*; reprinted
with permission of the author. 'The Case of Four and Twenty Blackbirds' by Neil Gaiman © 1984
by Neil Gaiman; first printed in *Knave*; reprinted in *Angels and Visitations* 1993; reprinted with
permission of Merrilee Heifetz Literary Agent on behalf of the author. 'Into Your Tent I'll Creep'
by Eric Frank Russell © 1957 by Street and Smith Publishing Inc for Astounding Science Fiction
1957; reprinted by permission of Laurence Pollinger Ltd. 'At Last, The True Story of
Frankenstein' by Harry Harrison; reprinted with permission of the author. 'We Can Remember
It For You Wholesale' and 'The Eyes Have It' by Philip K. Dick; reprinted by permission of the
author and the author's agents, Scovil Chichak Galen Literary Agency Inc. 'The Top 50 Things
I'd Do If I Ever Became an Evil Overlord' by Peter Anspach, from http://www.eviloverlord.com;
reprinted with permission of the author.

Cover design by The Point
Cover illustration by Dave Flanagan
Illustrations by Jackie Hill at 320 Design: 'Zero Hour' and 'Surfer and the Dreamcastle' – Jamel
Akib; 'Artificial Intelligence' – David Hopkins; 'The Fifty-First Dragon' – Alastair Graham; 'Into
Your Tent I'll Creep' – Alan Baker; 'We Can Remember It For You Wholesale' and 'Age of
Retirement' – Hashim Akib.
Typeset by Tek-Art, Croydon, Surrey
Printed and bound in the United Kingdom by Clays Ltd, St Ives plc

Contents

Space Spoofs

Introduction

Fantasy fiction has been popular for thousands of years. The epic poems of Homer, written around 1000 years BCE, are full of fantastic islands and incredible monsters. The Roman writer Lucan wrote of a voyage to the moon. Jonathan Swift's *Gulliver's Travels*, written in 1726, has the hero visiting strange lands (and flying islands!) peopled by midgets, giants and talking horses.

Science fiction is much more recent. It started with Mary Shelley's *Frankenstein*, first published in 1818. This was a completely new kind of story, where the monsters came, not from the outside, but from the dark heart of humanity itself.

There wasn't a word for it at first, even when writers like Jules Verne and H. G. Wells started to produce stories about alien invasions and amazing voyages to fantastic new worlds. These stories came to be known as 'scientific romances'. Later on, in the America of the 1920s and 1930s, magazines dedicated to such stories appeared on news stands by the score – *Amazing Stories*, *Weird Tales* and *Astounding Science Fiction* to name only a few. By now, there was a word for this new form of writing: 'scientifiction'. This obviously wasn't right, and after a few years the stories became known as science fiction.

Who are science fiction and fantasy for? As British sci-fi guru Brian Aldiss says, 'Science fiction is no more written for scientists than ghost stories are written for ghosts.' Science fiction and fantasy are now as much part of modern life as fast food and football. We are surrounded by computer and video games, superhero comics, cartoon series like *Pokémon*, and space operas like *Star Wars* and *Star Trek*. But it is the short story that has always been the test bed for new ideas. And in these stories, the great writers of science fiction and fantasy can challenge us and stretch our imaginations to the outer reaches of the universe and the darkest recesses of our own minds.

Accept the challenge. Enjoy the stories.

Live long and prosper.

Steve Barlow and Steve Skidmore

Zero Hour

Ray Bradbury

Ray Bradbury is a highly gifted writer who is equally at home with science-fiction and fantasy stories. His books include *The Silver Locusts* (also called *The Martian Chronicles*), *The Illustrated Man* and *Fahrenheit 451*.

It stands to reason that when aliens come to invade the Earth, they will arrive in spaceships the size of football stadiums and unleash death rays of inconceivable power to destroy the White House, etc. The wouldn't just quietly try to sneak in through the back door . . .

Would they?

Oh, it was to be so jolly! What a game! Such excitement they hadn't known in years. The children catapulted this way and that across the green lawns, shouting at each other, holding hands, flying in circles, climbing trees, laughing. Overhead the rockets flew, and beetle cars whispered by on the streets, but the children played on. Such fun, such **tremulous** joy, such tumbling and hearty screaming.

Mink ran into the house, all dirt and sweat. For her seven years she was loud and strong and definite. Her mother, Mrs Morris, hardly saw her as she yanked out drawers and rattled pans and tools into a large sack.

'Heavens, Mink, what's going on?'

'The most exciting game ever!' gasped Mink, pink-faced.

'Stop and get your breath,' said the mother.

'No, I'm all right,' gasped Mink. 'Okay I take these things, Mom?'

---

tremulous: trembling

'But don't dent them,' said Mrs Morris.

'Thank you, thank you!' cried Mink, and boom! she was gone, like a rocket.

Mrs Morris surveyed the fleeting tot. 'What's the name of the game?'

'Invasion!' said Mink. The door slammed

In every yard on the street children brought out knives and forks and pokers and old stovepipes and can openers.

It was an interesting fact that this fury and bustle occurred only among the younger children. The older ones, those ten years and more, disdained the affair and marched scornfully off on hikes or played a more dignified version of hide-and-seek on their own.

Meanwhile, parents came and went in chromium beetles. Repairmen came to repair the vacuum elevators in houses, to fix fluttering television sets or hammer upon stubborn food-delivery tubes. The adult civilisation passed and repassed the busy youngsters, jealous of the fierce energy of the wild tots, tolerantly amused at their flourishings, longing to join in themselves.

'This and this and *this*,' said Mink, instructing the others with their assorted spoons and wrenches. 'Do that, and bring *that* over here. No! Here, ninny! Right. Now, get back while I fix this.' Tongue in teeth, face wrinkled in thought. 'Like that. See?'

'Yayyyy!' shouted the kids.

Twelve-year-old Joseph Connors ran up.

'Go away,' said Mink straight at him.

'I wanna play,' said Joseph.

'Can't!' said Mink.

'Why not?'

'You'd just make fun of us.'

'Honest, I wouldn't.'

'No. We know you. Go away or we'll kick you.'

Another twelve-year-old boy whirred by on little motor skates. 'Hey, Joe! Come on! Let them sissies play!'

Joseph showed reluctance and a certain wistfulness.
'I *want* to play,' he said.
'You're old,' said Mink firmly.
'Not *that* old,' said Joe sensibly.
'You'd only laugh and spoil the Invasion.'
The boy on the motor skates made a rude lip noise.
'Come on, Joe! Them and their fairies! Nuts!'
Joseph walked off slowly. He kept looking back, all down the block.
Mink was already busy again. She made a kind of apparatus with her gathered equipment. She had appointed another little girl with a pad and pencil to take down notes in painful slow scribbles. Their voices rose and fell in the warm sunlight.
All around them the city hummed. The streets were lined with good green and peaceful trees. Only the wind made a conflict across the city, across the country, across the continent. In a thousand other cities there were trees and children and avenues, businessmen in their quiet offices taping their voices or watching televisors. Rockets hovered like darning needles in the blue sky. There was the universal, quiet **conceit** and easiness of men accustomed to peace, quite certain there would never be trouble again. Arm in arm, men all over earth were a united front. The perfect weapons were held in equal trust by all nations. A situation of incredibly beautiful balance had been brought about. There were no traitors among men – no unhappy ones, no disgruntled ones; therefore the world was based upon a stable ground. Sunlight illumined half the world and the trees drowsed in a tide of warm air.
Mink's mother, from her upstairs window, gazed down.
The children. She looked upon them and shook her

---

conceit: a fanciful idea

head. Well, they'd eat well, sleep well, and be in school on Monday. Bless their vigorous little bodies. She listened.

Mink talked earnestly to someone near the rose-bush – though there was no one there.

These odd children. And the little girl, what was her name? Anna? Anna took notes on a pad. First, Mink asked the rose-bush a question, then called the answer to Anna.

'Triangle,' said Mink.

'What's a tri,' said Anna with difficulty, 'angle?'

'Never mind,' said Mink.

'How you spell it?' asked Anna.

'T-r-i –' spelled Mink slowly, then snapped, 'Oh, spell it yourself!' She went on to other words. 'Beam,' she said.

'I haven't got tri,' said Anna, 'angle down yet!'

'Well, hurry, hurry!' cried Mink.

Mink's mother leaned out the upstairs window. 'A-n-g-l-e,' she spelled down at Anna.

'Oh, thanks, Mrs Morris,' said Anna.

'Certainly,' said Mink's mother and withdrew, laughing, to dust the hall with an electro-duster magnet.

The voices wavered on the shimmery air. 'Beam,' said Anna. Fading.

'Four-nine-seven-A-and-B-and-X,' said Mink, far away, seriously. 'And a fork and a string and a – hex-hex-agony – hexagon*al*!'

At lunch Mink gulped milk at one toss and was at the door. Her mother slapped the table.

'You sit right back down,' commanded Mrs Morris. 'Hot soup in a minute.' She poked a red button on the kitchen butler, and ten seconds later something landed with a bump in the rubber receiver. Mrs Morris opened it, took out a can with a pair of aluminium holders, unsealed it with a flick, and poured hot soup into a bowl.

During all this Mink fidgeted. 'Hurry, Mom! This is a matter of life and death! Aw –'

'I was the same way at your age. Always life and death.
I know.'

Mink banged away at the soup.

'Slow down,' said Mom.

'Can't,' said Mink. 'Drill's waiting for me.'

'Who's Drill? What a peculiar name,' said Mom.

'You don't know him,' said Mink.

'A new boy in the neighbourhood?' asked Mom.

'He's new all right,' said Mink. She started on her
second bowl.

'Which one is Drill?' asked Mom.

'He's around,' said Mink, evasively. 'You'll make fun.
Everybody pokes fun. Gee, darn.'

'Is Drill shy?'

'Yes. No. In a way. Gosh, Mom, I got to run if we want
to have the Invasion!'

'Who's invading what?'

'Martians invading Earth. Well, not exactly Martians.
They're – I don't know. From up.' She pointed with
her spoon.

'And *inside*,' said Mom, touching Mink's feverish brow.

Mink rebelled. 'You're laughing! You'll kill Drill
and everybody.'

'I didn't mean to,' said Mom. 'Drill's a Martian?'

'No. He's – well – maybe from Jupiter or Saturn or
Venus. Anyway, he's had a hard time.'

'I imagine.' Mrs Morris hid her mouth behind
her hand.

'They couldn't figure a way to attack Earth.'

'We're **impregnable**,' said Mom in mock seriousness.

'That's the word Drill used! Impreg – That was the
word, Mom.'

'My, my, Drill's a brilliant little boy. Two-bit words.'

'They couldn't figure a way to attack, Mom. Drill says –

---

impregnable: safe from attack

he says in order to make a good fight you got to have a new way of surprising people. That way you win. And he says also you got to have help from your enemy.'

'A fifth column,' said Mom.

'Yeah. That's what Drill said. And they couldn't figure a way to surprise Earth or get help.'

'No wonder. We're pretty darn strong,' Mom laughed, cleaning up. Mink sat there, staring at the table, seeing what she was talking about.

'Until, one day,' whispered Mink **melodramatically**, 'they thought of children!'

'*Well!*' said Mrs Morris brightly.

'And they thought of how grown-ups are so busy they never look under rose-bushes or on lawns!'

'Only for snails and fungus.'

'And then there's something about dim-dims.'

'Dim-dims?'

'Dimens-shuns.'

'Dimensions?'

'Four of 'em! And there's something about kids under nine and imagination. It's real funny to hear Drill talk.'

Mrs Morris was tired. 'Well, it must be funny. You're keeping Drill waiting now. It's getting late in the day and, if you want to have your Invasion before your supper bath, you'd better jump.'

'Do I have to take a bath?' growled Mink.

'You do. Why is it children hate water? No matter what age you live in children hate water behind the ears!'

'Drill says I won't have to take baths,' said Mink.

'Oh, he does, does he?'

'He told all the kids that. No more baths. And we can stay up till ten o'clock and go to two televisor shows on Saturday 'stead of one!'

---

melodramatically: with a lot of drama, sensationally

'Well, Mr Drill better mind his p's and q's. I'll call up his mother and –'

Mink went to the door. 'We're having trouble with guys like Pete Britz and Dale Jerrick. They're growing up. They make fun. They're worse than parents. They just won't believe in Drill. They're so snooty, 'cause they're growing up. You'd think they'd know better. They were little only a coupla years ago. I hate them worst. We'll kill them *first*.'

'Your father and I last?'

'Drill says you're dangerous. Know why? 'Cause you don't believe in Martians! They're going to let *us* run the world. Well, not just us, but the kids over in the next block, too. I might be queen.' She opened the door.

'Mom?'

'Yes?'

'What's lodge-ick?'

'Logic? Why, dear, logic is knowing what things are true and not true.'

'He *mentioned* that,' said Mink. 'And what's im-pres-sion-able?' It took her a minute to say it.

'Why, it means –' Her mother looked at the floor, laughing gently. 'It means – to be a child, dear.'

'Thanks for lunch!' Mink ran out, then stuck her head back in. 'Mom, I'll be sure you won't be hurt much, really!'

'Well, thanks,' said Mom.

Slam went the door.

At four o'clock the audio-visor buzzed. Mrs Morris flipped the tab. 'Hello, Helen!' she said in welcome.

'Hello, Mary. How are things in New York?'

'Fine. How are things in Scranton? You look tired.'

'So do you. The children. Underfoot,' said Helen.

Mrs Morris sighed. 'My Mink too. The super-Invasion.'

Helen laughed. 'Are your kids playing that game too?'

'Lord, yes. Tomorrow it'll be geometrical jacks and motorised hopscotch. Were we this bad when we were kids in '48?'

'Worse. Japs and Nazis. Don't know how my parents put up with me. Tomboy.'

'Parents learn to shut their ears.'

A silence.

'What's wrong, Mary?' asked Helen.

Mrs Morris's eyes were half-closed; her tongue slid slowly, thoughtfully, over her lower lip. 'Eh?' She jerked. 'Oh, nothing. Just thought about *that*. Shutting ears and such. Never mind. Where were we?'

'My boy Tim's got a crush on some guy named – *Drill*, I think it was.'

'Must be a new password. Mink likes him too.'

'Didn't know it had got as far as New York. Word of mouth, I imagine. Looks like a scrap drive. I talked to Josephine and she said her kids – that's in Boston – are wild on this new game. It's sweeping the country.'

At this moment Mink trotted into the kitchen to gulp a glass of water. Mrs Morris turned. 'How're things going?'

'Almost finished,' said Mink.

'Swell,' said Mrs Morris. 'What's *that*?'

'A yo-yo,' said Mink. 'Watch.'

She flung the yo-yo down its string. Reaching the end it – it vanished.

'See?' said Mink. 'Ope!' Dibbling her finger, she made the yo-yo reappear and zip up the string.

'Do that again,' said her mother.

'Can't. Zero hour's five o'clock! 'By.' Mink exited, zipping her yo-yo.

On the audio-visor, Helen laughed. 'Tim brought one of those yo-yos in this morning, but when I got curious he said he wouldn't show it to me, and when I tried to work it, finally, it wouldn't work.'

'You're not *impressionable*,' said Mrs Morris.

'What?'

'Never mind. Something I thought of. Can I help you, Helen?'

'I wanted to get that black-and-white cake recipe –'

The hour drowsed by. The day waned. The sun lowered in the peaceful blue sky. Shadows lengthened on the green lawns. The laughter and excitement continued. One little girl ran away, crying. Mrs Morris came out the front door.

'Mink, was that Peggy Ann crying?'

Mink was bent over in the yard, near the rose-bush. 'Yeah. She's a scarebaby. We won't let her play, now. She's getting too old to play. I guess she grew up all of a sudden.'

'Is that why she cried? Nonsense. Give me a civil answer, young lady, or inside you come!'

Mink whirled in consternation, mixed with irritation. 'I can't quit now. It's almost time. I'll be good. I'm sorry.'

'Did you hit Peggy Ann?'

'No, honest. You ask her. It was something – well, she's just a scaredy pants.'

The ring of children drew in around Mink where she scowled at her work with spoons and a kind of square-shaped arrangement of hammers and pipes. 'There and there,' murmured Mink.

'What's wrong?' said Mrs Morris.

'Drill's stuck. Halfway. If we could only get him all the way through, it'd be easier. Then all the others could come through after him.'

'Can I help?'

'No'm, thanks. I'll fix it.'

'All right. I'll call you for your bath in half an hour. I'm tired of watching you.'

She went in and sat in the electric relaxing chair, sipping a little beer from a half-empty glass. The chair massaged her back. Children, children. Children and love and hate, side by side. Sometimes children loved you, hated you – all in half a second. Strange children, did they ever forget or forgive the whippings and the harsh, strict words of command? She wondered. How can you ever forget or forgive those over and above you, those tall and silly dictators?

Time passed. A curious, waiting silence came upon the street, deepening.

Five o'clock. A clock sang softly somewhere in the house in a quiet, musical voice: 'Five o'clock – five o'clock. Time's a-wasting. Five o'clock,' and purred away into silence.

Zero hour.

Mrs Morris chuckled in her throat. Zero hour.

A beetle car hummed into the driveway. Mr Morris. Mrs Morris smiled. Mr Morris got out of the beetle, locked it, and called hello to Mink at her work. Mink ignored him. He laughed and stood for a moment watching the children. Then he walked up the front steps.

'Hello, darling.'

'Hello, Henry.'

She strained forward on the edge of the chair, listening. The children were silent. Too silent.

He emptied his pipe, refilled it. 'Swell day. Makes you glad to be alive.'

Buzz.

'What's that?' asked Henry.

'I don't know.' She got up suddenly, her eyes widening. She was going to say something. She stopped it. Ridiculous. Her nerves jumped. 'Those children haven't anything dangerous out there, have they?' she said.

'Nothing but pipes and hammers. Why?'

'Nothing electrical?'

'Heck, no,' said Henry. 'I looked.'

She walked to the kitchen. The buzzing continued. 'Just the same, you'd better go tell them to quit. It's after five. Tell them –' Her eyes widened and narrowed. 'Tell them to put off their Invasion until tomorrow.' She laughed, nervously.

The buzzing grew louder.

'What are they up to? I'd better go look, all right.'

The explosion!

The house shook with dull sound. There were other explosions in other yards on other streets.

Involuntarily, Mrs Morris screamed. 'Up this way!' she cried senselessly, knowing no sense, no reason. Perhaps she saw something from the corners of her eyes; perhaps she smelled a new odour or heard a new noise. There was no time to argue with Henry to convince him. Let him think her insane. Yes, insane! Shrieking, she ran upstairs. He ran after her to see what she was up to. 'In the attic!' she screamed. 'That's where it is!' It was only a poor excuse to get him in the attic in time. Oh, God – in time!

Another explosion outside. The children screamed with delight, as if at a great fireworks display.

'It's not in the attic!' cried Henry. 'It's outside!'

'No, no!' Wheezing, gasping, she fumbled at the attic door. 'I'll show you. Hurry! I'll show you!'

They tumbled into the attic. She slammed the door, locked it, took the key, threw it into a far, cluttered corner. She was babbling wild stuff now. It came out of her. All the subconscious suspicion and fear that had gathered secretly all afternoon and fermented like a wine in her. All the little revelations and knowledges and sense that had bothered her all day and which she had logically and carefully and sensibly rejected and censored. Now it exploded in her and shook her to bits.

'There, there,' she said, sobbing against the door. 'We're safe until tonight. Maybe we can sneak out. Maybe we can escape!'

Henry blew up too, but for another reason. 'Are you crazy? Why'd you throw that key away? Damn it, honey!'

'Yes, yes, I'm crazy, if it helps, but stay here with me!'

'I don't know how in hell I *can* get out!'

'Quiet. They'll hear us. Oh, God, they'll find us soon enough –'

Below them, Mink's voice. The husband stopped. There was a great universal humming and sizzling, a screaming and giggling. Downstairs the audio-televisor buzzed and buzzed insistently, alarmingly, violently. *Is that Helen calling?* thought Mrs Morris. *And is she calling about what I think she's calling about?*

Footsteps came into the house. Heavy footsteps.

'Who's coming in my house?' demanded Henry angrily. 'Who's tramping around down there?'

Heavy feet. Twenty, thirty, forty, fifty of them. Fifty persons crowding into the house. The humming. The giggling of the children. 'This way!' cried Mink, below.

'Who's downstairs?' roared Henry. 'Who's there!'

'Hush. Oh, nononononono!' said his wife weakly, holding him. 'Please, be quiet. They might go away.'

'Mom?' called Mink. 'Dad?' A pause. 'Where are you?'

Heavy footsteps, heavy, heavy, *very heavy* footsteps, came up the stairs. Mink leading them.

'Mom?' A hesitation. 'Dad?' A waiting, a silence.

Humming. Footsteps towards the attic. Mink's first.

They trembled together in silence in the attic, Mr and Mrs Morris. For some reason the electric humming, the queer cold light suddenly visible under the door crack, the strange odour and the alien sound of eagerness in Mink's voice finally got through to Henry Morris too. He stood, shivering, in the dark silence, his wife beside him.

'Mom! Dad!'

Footsteps. A little humming sound. The attic lock melted. The door opened. Mink peered inside, tall blue shadows behind her.

'Peekaboo,' said Mink.

Feeding Time
James E. Gunn

James E. Gunn isn't the most famous sci-fi writer around, but he deserves to be better known for his tales like *The Immortals* and *The Joymakers*.

In this story, he shows that he has a wicked sense of humour – and maybe, that he doesn't have much time for psychiatrists . . .

Angela woke up with the sickening realisation that today was feeding time. She slipped out of bed, hurried to the desk, and leafed nervously through her appointment book. She laughed with relief; it was all right – today was her appointment.

Angela took only 45 minutes for make-up and dressing: it was feeding time. As she descended in the elevator, walked swiftly through the lobby, and got into a taxi, she didn't even notice the eyes that stopped and swivelled after her: feeding time.

Angela was haunted by a zoo.

She was also haunted by men, but this was understandable. She was the kind of blond, blue-eyed angel men pray to – or for – and she had the kind of measurements – 36-26-36 – that make men want to take up mathematics.

But Angela had no time for men – not today. Angela was haunted by a zoo, and it was feeding time.

Dr Bachman had a ·grey-bearded, pink-skinned, blue-eyed kindliness that was his greatest stock in trade. Underneath, there was something else not quite so kindly which had been influential in his choice of

professions. Now, for a moment, his professional mask –
his **persona**, as the **Jungians** call it – slipped aside.

'A zoo?' he repeated, his voice clear, deep, and
cultured, with just a trace of accent; Viennese
without a doubt. He caught himself quickly. 'A
zoo. Exactly.'

'Well, not exactly a zoo,' said Angela, pursing her red
lips thoughtfully at the ceiling. 'At least not an ordinary
zoo. It's really only one animal – if you could call him
an animal.'

'What do you call him?'

'Oh, I never call him,' Angela said quickly, giving
a delicious little shiver. 'He might come.'

'Hm-m-m,' hm-m-med Dr Bachman neutrally.

'But you don't mean that,' Angela said softly. 'You mean
if he isn't an animal, what is he? What he is – is a monster.'

'What kind of monster?' Dr Bachman asked calmly.

Angela turned on one elbow and looked over the back
of the couch at the **psychoanalyst.**

'You say that as if you met monsters every day. But then
I guess you do.' She sighed sympathetically. 'It's
a dangerous business, being a psychiatrist.'

'Dangerous?' Dr Bachman repeated **querulously**,
caught off guard a second time. 'What do you mean?'

'Oh, the people you meet – all the strange ones – and
their problems –'

'Yes, yes, of course,' he said hurriedly. 'But about
the monster?'

---

persona: Jung's term for a person's way of dealing with the world
Jungian: according to Jung's theories; Carl Gustav Jung was a Swiss
psychologist
psychoanalyst: a person who investigates and treats mental or
nervous diseases by helping the patient remember ideas hidden in
the patient's mind
querulously: in a complaining way

'Yes, doctor,' Angela said in her obedient tone and composed herself again on the couch. She looked at the corner of the ceiling as if she could see him clinging there. 'He's not a nightmare monster, though he's frightening enough. He's too real; there are no blurred edges. He has purple fur – short, rather like the fur on some spiders – and four legs, not evenly distributed like a dog's or a cat's but grouped together at the bottom. They're very strong – much stronger than they need to be. He can jump fifteen feet straight up into the air.'

She turned again to look at Dr Bachman. 'Are you getting all this?'

Hastily, the psychoanalyst turned his notebook away, but Angela had already caught a glimpse of his doodling.

'Goodie!' she said, clapping her hands in delight. 'You're drawing a picture.'

'Yes, yes,' he said grumpily. 'Go on.'

'Well, he has only two arms. He has six fingers on each hand, and they're flexible, as if they had no bones in them. They're elastic too. They can stretch way out – as if to pick fruit that grows on a very tall vine.'

'A vegetarian,' said Dr Bachman, making his small joke.

'Oh, no, doctor!' Angela said, her eyes wide. 'He eats everything, but meat is what he likes the best. His face is almost human except it's green. He has very sharp teeth.' She shuddered. 'Very sharp. Am I going too fast?'

'Don't worry about me!' snapped the psychoanalyst. 'It is your subconscious we are exploring, and it must go at its own speed.'

'Oh, dear,' Angela said with resignation. 'The subconscious. It's going to be another one of those.'

'You don't believe this nightmare has any objective reality?' Dr Bachman asked sharply.

'That would make me insane, wouldn't it? Well, I guess there's no help for it. That's what I think.'

Dr Bachman tugged thoughtfully at his beard. 'I see. Let's go back. How did this illusion begin?'

'I think it began with the **claustrophobia**.'

Dr Bachman shrugged. 'A **morbid** fear of confined places is not unusual.'

'It is when you're out in the open air. The fear had no relationship to my surroundings. All of a sudden, I'd feel like I was in a fairly large room which had a tremendous weight of rock or masonry above it. It was in the midst of a crowd of people. For moments it became so real that my actual surroundings faded out.'

'But the feeling came and went.'

'Yes. Then came the smell. It was a distinctive odour – musty and strong like the lion house in the winter, only wrong, somehow. But it made me think of the zoo.'

'Naturally you were the only one who smelled it.'

'That's right. I was self-conscious, at first. I tried to drown out the odour with perfume, but that didn't help. Then I realised that no one else seemed to smell it. Like the claustrophobia, it came and went. But each time it returned it was stronger. Finally I went to a psychiatrist – a Dr Aber.'

'That was before the illusion became visual?'

'That was sort of Dr Aber's fault – my seeing the monster, I mean.'

'It is to be expected,' Dr Bachman said.

'When nothing else worked, Dr Aber tried hypnosis. "Reach into your subconscious," he said. "Open the door to the past!" Well, I reached out. I opened the door. And that's when it happened.'

'What happened?' Dr Bachman leaned forward.

'I saw the monster.'

'Oh,' He leaned back again, disappointed.

---

claustrophobia: a fear of confined places
morbid: unwholesome

'People were close, but the monster was closer. The odour was stifling as he stared through the door – and saw me. I slammed the door shut, but it was too late. The door was there. I knew it could be opened. And he knew it could be opened. Now I was really afraid.'

'Afraid?'

'That the monster might get through the door.'

The psychoanalyst tugged at his beard. 'You have an explanation for this illusion?'

'You won't laugh?'

'Certainly not!'

'I think, through some strange accident of time, I've become linked to a zoo that will exist in the distant future. The monster – wasn't born on Earth. He's an alien – from Jupiter, perhaps, although I don't think so. Through the door I can see part of a sign; I can read this much.'

Angela turned and took the notebook from his surprised fingers and printed quickly:

M'RA
(Larmis
Nativ)
Vega

'Just like in the zoo,' she said, handing the book back. 'There's a star named Vega.'

'Yes,' said the psychoanalyst heavily. 'And you are afraid that this . . . alien will get through the door and –'

'That's it. He can open it now, you see. He can't exist here; that would be impossible. But something from the present can exist in the future. And the monster gets hungry – for meat.'

'For meat?' Dr Bachman repeated, frowning.

'Every few weeks,' Angela said, shivering, 'it's feeding time.'

Dr Bachman tugged at his beard, preparing the swift, feline stroke which would lay bare the traumatic relationship at the root of the **neurosis**. He said, incisively, 'The monster resembles your father, is that not so?'

It was Angela's turn to frown. 'That's what Dr Aber said. I'd never have noticed it on my own. There might be a slight resemblance.'

'This Dr Aber – he did you no good?'

'Oh, I wouldn't want you to think that,' Angela protested quickly. 'He helped. But the help was – temporary, if you know what I mean.'

'And you would like something more permanent.'

'That would be nice,' Angela admitted. 'But I'm afraid it's too much to hope for.'

'No. It will take time, but eventually we will work these subconscious repressions into your conscious mind, where they will be cleansed of their neurotic value.'

'You think it's all in my head?' Angela said wistfully.

'Certainly,' the psychoanalyst said briskly. 'Let us go over the progress of the illusion once more: First came the claustrophobia, then the smell, then, through Dr Aber's bung . . . treatment, I should say, the dreams –'

'Oh, not dreams, doctor,' Angela corrected. 'When I sleep, I don't dream of monsters. I dream' – she blushed prettily – 'of men. The thing in the zoo – I can see him whenever I close my eyes.' She shivered. 'He's getting impatient.'

'Hungry?'

Angela beamed at him. 'Yes. It's almost feeding time. He gets fed, of course. By the keeper, I suppose. But that's just grains and fruits and things like that. And he gets hungry for meat.'

'And then?'

'He opens the door.'

---

neurosis: a mental disturbance

'And I suppose he sticks through his elastic fingers.'

Angela gave him a look of pure gratitude. 'That's right.'

'And you're afraid that one day he will get hungry enough to eat you.'

'That's it, I guess. Wouldn't you be – afraid, that is? There's all the legends about dragons and Minotaurs and creatures like that. They always preferred a diet of young virgins; and where there's all that talk –'

'If that were your only concern,' Dr Bachman commented dryly, 'it seems to me that you could make yourself ineligible with no great difficulty.'

Angela giggled. 'Why, doctor! What a suggestion!'

'Hm-m-m,' hm-m-med the psychoanalyst. 'So! To return. Every few weeks comes feeding time and you, feeling nervous and afraid, come to me for help.'

'You put it so well.'

'And now it's feeding time.'

'That's right.' Angela's nostrils dilated suddenly. 'He's getting close to the door. Don't you smell him, doctor?'

Dr Bachman sniffed once and snorted. 'Certainly not. Now tell me about your father.'

'Well,' Angela began reluctantly, 'he believed in **reincarnation** –'

'No, no,' the psychoanalyst said impatiently. 'The important things. How you felt about him when you were a little girl. What he said to you. How you hated your mother.'

'I'm afraid there won't be time. He's got one of his hands on the door already.'

Despite himself, Dr Bachman glanced back over his shoulder. 'The monster?' His beard twitched nervously. 'Nonsense. About your father –'

'The door's opened!' Angela cried out. 'I'm scared, doctor. It's feeding time!'

---

reincarnation: being born again in another body or form

'I won't be tricked again,' the psychoanalyst said sternly. 'If we're to get anywhere with this analysis, I must have complete –'

'Doctor! Watch out! The fingers – Dr Bachman! Doctor! Doc –!'

Angela sighed. It was a strange sigh, half hopelessness and half relief. She picked up her **purse**.

'Doctor?' she said tentatively to the empty room.

She stood up, sniffing the air gingerly. The odour was gone. So was Dr Bachman.

She walked towards the door. 'Doctor?' she tried once more.

There was no answer. There never had been an answer, not from seventeen psychiatrists. There was no doubt about it. The monster did like psychiatrists.

It was a truly terrifying situation she was in, certainly through no fault of her own, and a girl had to do the best she could. She could console herself with the thought that the monster would never take her for food.

She was the trapdoor it needed into this world. Eat her, and feeding time was over.

She was perfectly safe.

As long as she didn't run out of psychiatrists.

---

purse: handbag

To Serve Man
Damon Knight

Damon Knight is best known as a critic. He was one of the first writers to take science fiction seriously, in his book *In Search of Wonder*. He has edited many collections of science-fiction and fantasy stories. He founded a writers' group called the Science Fiction Writers of America (SFWA). Apart from all that, he writes a pretty good story himself.

As for *this* story – it may remind you of an old saying: 'There's no such thing as a free lunch . . .'

The Kanamit were not very pretty, it's true. They looked something like pigs and something like people, and that is not an attractive combination. Seeing them for the first time shocked you; that was their handicap. When a thing with the countenance of a fiend comes from the stars and offers a gift, you are disinclined to accept.

I don't know what we expected interstellar visitors to look like – those who thought about it at all, that is. Angels, perhaps, or something too alien to be really awful. Maybe that's why we were all so horrified and repelled when they landed in their great ships and we saw what they really were like.

The Kanamit were short and very hairy – thick, bristly brown-grey hair all over their abominably plump bodies. Their noses were snoutlike and their eyes small, and they had thick hands of three fingers each. They wore green leather harness and green shorts, but I think the shorts were a concession to our notions of public decency. The garments were quite modishly cut, with slash pockets and half-belts in the back. The Kanamit had a sense of humour, anyhow.

There were three of them at this session of the UN, and, Lord, I can't tell you how queer it looked to see them there in the middle of a solemn **plenary** session – three fat piglike creatures in green harness and shorts, sitting at the long table below the podium, surrounded by the packed arcs of delegates from every nation. They sat correctly upright, politely watching each speaker. Their flat ears drooped over the earphones. Later on, I believe, they learned every human language, but at this time they knew only French and English.

They seemed perfectly at ease – and that, along with their humour, was a thing that tended to make me like them. I was in the minority; I didn't think they were trying to put anything over.

The delegate from Argentina got up and said that his government was interested in the demonstration of a new cheap power source, which the Kanamit had made at the previous session, but that the Argentine government could not commit itself as to its future policy without a much more thorough examination.

It was what all the delegates were saying, but I had to pay particular attention to Señor Valdes, because he tended to sputter and his diction was bad. I got through the translation all right, with only one or two momentary hesitations, and then switched to the Polish–English line to hear how Gregori was doing with Janciewicz. Janciewicz was the cross Gregori had to bear, just as Valdes was mine.

Janciewicz repeated the previous remarks with a few ideological variations, and then the Secretary-General recognised the delegate from France, who introduced

---

UN: United Nations
plenary: with all the members present

Dr Denis Lévèque, the criminologist, and a great deal of complicated equipment was wheeled in.

Dr Lévèque remarked that the question in many people's minds had been aptly expressed by the delegate from the **USSR** at the preceding session, when he demanded, 'What is the motive of the Kanamit? What is their purpose in offering us these **unprecedented** gifts, while asking nothing in return?'

The doctor then said, 'At the request of several delegates and with the full consent of our guests, the Kanamit, my associates and I have made a series of tests upon the Kanamit with the equipment which you see before you. These tests will now be repeated.'

A murmur ran through the chamber. There was a **fusillade** of flashbulbs, and one of the TV cameras moved up to focus on the instrument board of the doctor's equipment. At the same time, the huge television screen behind the podium lighted up, and we saw the blank faces of two dials, each with its pointer resting at zero, and a strip of paper tape with a stylus point resting against it.

The doctor's assistants were fastening wires to the temples of one of the Kanamit, wrapping a canvas-covered rubber tube around his forearm, and taping something to the palm of his right hand.

In the screen, we saw the paper tape begin to move while the stylus traced a slow zigzag pattern along it. One of the needles began to jump rhythmically; the other flipped over and stayed there, wavering slightly.

'These are the standard instruments for testing the truth of a statement,' said Dr Lévèque. 'Our first object, since the **physiology** of the Kanamit is unknown to us,

---

USSR: Union of Soviet Socialist Republics
unprecedented: never happened before
fusillade: a continuous firing (usually of firearms) at the same time
physiology: the science of the process of life in plants and animals

was to determine whether or not they react to these tests as human beings do. We will now repeat one of the many experiments which were made in the endeavour to discover this.'

He pointed to the first dial. 'This instrument registers the subject's heartbeat. This shows the electrical **conductivity** of the skin in the palm of his hand, a measure of perspiration, which increases under stress. 'And this' – pointing to the tape-and-stylus device – 'shows the pattern and intensity of the electrical waves **emanating** from his brain. It has been shown, with human subjects, that all these readings vary markedly depending upon whether the subject is speaking the truth.'

He picked up two large pieces of cardboard, one red and one black. The red one was a square about three feet on a side; the black was a rectangle three and a half feet long. He addressed himself to the Kanama.

'Which of these is longer than the other?'

'The red,' said the Kanama.

Both needles leaped wildly, and so did the line on the unrolling tape.

'I shall repeat the question,' said the doctor. 'Which of these is longer than the other?'

'The black,' said the creature.

This time the instruments continued in their normal rhythm.

'How did you come to this planet?' asked the doctor.

'Walked,' replied the Kanama.

Again the instruments responded, and there was a subdued ripple of laughter in the chamber.

'Once more,' said the doctor. 'How did you come to this planet?'

---

conductivity: the ability of an object to lead or guide something through itself
emanating: coming out of

'In a spaceship,' said the Kanama, and the instruments did not jump.

The doctor again faced the delegates. 'Many such experiments were made,' he said, 'and my colleagues and myself are satisfied that the mechanisms are effective. Now' – he turned to the Kanama – 'I shall ask our distinguished guest to reply to the question put at the last session by the delegate of the USSR – namely, what is the motive of the Kanamit people in offering these great gifts to the people of Earth?'

The Kanama rose. Speaking this time in English, he said, 'On my planet there is a saying, "There are more riddles in a stone than in a philosopher's head." The motives of intelligent beings, though they may at times appear obscure, are simple things compared to the complex workings of the natural universe. Therefore I hope that the people of Earth will understand, and believe, when I tell you that our mission upon your planet is simply this – to bring to you the peace and plenty which we ourselves enjoy, and which we have in the past brought to other races through the galaxy. When your world has no more hunger, no more war, no more needless suffering, that will be our reward.'

And the needles had not jumped once.

The delegate from the Ukraine jumped to his feet, asking to be recognised, but the time was up and the Secretary-General closed the session.

I met Gregori as we were leaving the chamber. His face was red with excitement. 'Who promoted that circus?' he demanded.

'The tests looked genuine to me,' I told him.

'A circus!' he said vehemently. 'A second-rate farce! If they were genuine, Peter, why was debate stifled?'

'There'll be time for debate tomorrow, surely.'

'Tomorrow the doctor and his instruments will be back in Paris. Plenty of things can happen before tomorrow. In the name of sanity, man, how can anybody trust a thing that looks as if it ate the baby?'

I was a little annoyed. I said, 'Are you sure you're not more worried about their politics than their appearance?'

He said, 'Bah,' and went away.

The next day reports began to come in from government laboratories all over the world where the Kanamit's power source was being tested. They were wildly enthusiastic. I don't understand such things myself, but it seemed that those little metal boxes would give more electrical power than an atomic pile, for next to nothing and nearly for ever. And it was said that they were so cheap to manufacture that everybody in the world could have one of his own. In the early afternoon there were reports that seventeen countries had already begun to set up factories to turn them out.

The next day the Kanamit turned up with plans and specimens of a gadget that would increase the fertility of any arable land by 60 to 100 per cent. It speeded the formation of nitrates in the soil, or something. There was nothing in the newscasts any more but stories about the Kanamit. The day after that, they dropped their bombshell.

'You now have potentially unlimited power and increased food supply,' said one of them. He pointed with his three-fingered hand to an instrument that stood on the table before him. It was a box on a tripod, with a parabolic reflector on the front of it. 'We offer you today a third gift which is at least as important as the first two.'

He beckoned to the TV men to roll their cameras into close-up position. Then he picked up a large sheet of cardboard covered with drawings and English lettering. We saw it on the large screen above the podium; it was all clearly legible.

'We are informed that this broadcast is being relayed throughout your world,' said the Kanama. 'I wish that everyone who has equipment for taking photographs from television screens would use it now.'

The Secretary-General leaned forward and asked a question sharply, but the Kanama ignored him.

'This device,' he said, 'generates a field in which no explosive, of whatever nature, can detonate.'

There was an uncomprehending silence.

The Kanama said, 'It cannot now be suppressed. If one nation has it, all must have it.' When nobody seemed to understand, he explained bluntly, 'There will be no more war.'

That was the biggest news of the millennium, and it was perfectly true. It turned out that the explosions the Kanama was talking about included gasoline and diesel explosions. They had simply made it impossible for anybody to mount or equip a modern army.

We could have gone back to bows and arrows, of course, but that wouldn't have satisfied the military. Besides, there wouldn't be any reason to make war. Every nation would soon have everything.

Nobody ever gave another thought to those lie-detector experiments, or asked the Kanamit what their politics were. Gregori was put out; he had nothing to prove his suspicions.

I quit my job with the UN a few months later, because I foresaw that it was going to die under me anyhow. UN business was booming at the time, but after a year or so there was going to be nothing for it to do. Every nation on Earth was well on the way to being completely self-supporting; they weren't going to need much **arbitration**.

I accepted a position as translator with the Kanamit Embassy, and it was there that I ran into Gregori again. I was glad to see him, but I couldn't imagine what he was doing there.

---

arbitration: decision-making by a judge

'I thought you were on the opposition,' I said. 'Don't tell me you're convinced the Kanamit are all right.'

He looked rather shamefaced. 'They're not what they look, anyhow,' he said.

It was as much of a concession as he could decently make, and I invited him down to the embassy lounge for a drink. It was an intimate kind of place, and he grew confidential over the second daiquiri.

'They fascinate me,' he said. 'I hate them instinctively still – that hasn't changed – but I can evaluate it. You were right, obviously; they mean us nothing but good. But do you know' – he leaned across the table – 'the question of the Soviet delegate was never answered.'

I am afraid I snorted.

'No, really,' he said. 'They told us what they wanted to do – "to bring to you the peace and plenty which we ourselves enjoy". But they didn't say why.'

'Why do missionaries –'

'Missionaries be damned!' he said angrily. 'Missionaries have a religious motive. If these creatures have a religion they haven't once mentioned it. What's more, they didn't send a missionary group; they send a **diplomatic delegation** – a group representing the will and policy of their whole people. Now just what have the Kanamit, as a people or a nation, got to gain from our welfare?'

I said, 'Cultural –'

'Cultural cabbage soup! No, it's something less obvious than that, something obscure that belongs to their psychology and not to ours. But trust me, Peter, there is no such thing as a completely disinterested **altruism**. In one way or another, they have something to gain.'

---

diplomatic delegation: a group of people who manage relations between states

altruism: the principle of living and acting for others

'And that's why you're here,' I said. 'To try to find out what it is.'

'Correct. I wanted to get on one of the ten-year exchange groups to their home planet, but I couldn't; the quota was filled a week after they made the announcement. This is the next best thing. I'm studying their language, and you know that language reflects the basic assumptions of the people who use it. I've got a fair command of the spoken lingo already. It's not hard, really, and there are hints in it. Some of the idioms are quite similar to English. I'm sure I'll get the answer eventually.'

'More power,' I said, and we went back to work.

I saw Gregori frequently from then on, and he kept me posted about his progress. He was highly excited about a month after that first meeting; said he'd got hold of a book of the Kanamit's and was trying to puzzle it out. They wrote in ideographs, worse than Chinese, but he was determined to fathom it if it took him years. He wanted my help.

Well, I was interested in spite of myself, for I knew it would be a long job. We spent some evenings together, working with material from Kanamit bulletin boards and so forth, and with the extremely limited English– Kanamit dictionary they issued to the staff. My conscience bothered me about the stolen book, but gradually I became absorbed by the problem. Languages are my field, after all. I couldn't help being fascinated.

We got the title worked out in a few weeks. It was *How to Serve Man*, evidently a handbook they were giving out to new Kanamit members of the embassy staff. They had new ones in, all the time now, a shipload about once a month; they were opening all kinds of research laboratories, clinics and so on. If there was anybody on Earth besides Gregori who still distrusted those people, he must have been somewhere in the middle of Tibet.

It was astonishing to see the changes that had been wrought in less than a year. There were no more standing armies, no more shortages, no unemployment. When you picked up a newspaper you didn't see H-BOMB or SATELLITE leaping out at you; the news was always good. It was a hard thing to get used to. The Kanamit were working on human biochemistry, and it was known around the embassy that they were nearly ready to announce methods of making our race taller and stronger and healthier – practically a race of supermen – and they had a potential cure for heart disease and cancer.

I didn't see Gregori for a fortnight after we finished working out the title of the book; I was on a long-overdue vacation in Canada. When I got back, I was shocked by the change in his appearance.

'What on earth is wrong, Gregori?' I asked. 'You look like the very devil.'

'Come down to the lounge.'

I went with him, and he gulped a stiff Scotch as if he needed it.

'Come on, man, what's the matter?' I urged.

'The Kanamit have put me on the passenger list for the next exchange ship,' he said. 'You too, otherwise I wouldn't be talking to you.'

'Well,' I said, 'but –'

'They're not **altruists**.'

I tried to reason with him. I pointed out they'd made Earth a paradise compared to what it was before. He only shook his head.

Then I said, 'Well, what about those lie-detector tests?'

'A farce,' he replied, without heat. 'I said so at the time, you fool. They told the truth, though, as far as it went.'

---

altruist: a person who lives or acts for others

'And the book?' I demanded, annoyed. 'What about that – *How to Serve Man*? That wasn't put there for you to read. They *mean* it. How do you explain that?'

'I've read the first paragraph of that book,' he said. 'Why do you suppose I haven't slept for a week?'

I said, 'Well?' and he smiled a curious, twisted smile.

'It's a cookbook,' he said.

Artificial Intelligence
Malorie Blackman

Malorie Blackman is an award-winning British writer for children. Before the success of her computer-based novel *Hacker*, Malorie studied computer science and worked as a database manager. A lot of her work deals with hi-tech innovations. Her book, *Pig-heart Boy*, explores the world of transplants and has been made into a television series.

In *Artificial Intelligence*, Malorie asks the question: if a robot were given human emotions and feelings, would it know it was a robot?

'Come on, Mum, you *must* know.'

'Claire, how many more times?' Mum said, exasperated. 'I don't know what your dad is working on. You know he doesn't like to show us what he's doing until it's completely finished and he's totally happy with it.'

'But what d'you think it might be?' I persisted. 'I mean, why did he need all that information from me? And why did he scan my mind for my brain patterns? What's that got to do with . . .?'

'Claire, read my lips – I DON'T KNOW.' Mum raised an impatient, grey hand to swot away an irritating bluebottle. She made contact and it fell dead at her feet.

I decided not to push it. From the sparks practically flying out of Mum's eyes, it was obvious she was beginning to get more than annoyed.

'You dad said he'd show us what he's been working on later today and he will. Until then you'll just have to wait,' Mum said, calming down slightly. She picked up the fly and dropped it into the bin by her armchair.

I stood up.

'Where're you going?' Mum asked.

'To do my homework.'

'To do your homework or to play on the Cybanet?' Mum asked drily.

'I don't *play* on the Cybanet. I work, I research, I gather data, I further my education . . .'

'But mostly you play!' laughed Mum.

I couldn't help laughing as well – because it was true!

'I'm not going to play now though. I'm going to talk to my pen pal,' I said.

'You've found one at last, have you?'

'Mum, where've you been? I've had a pen pal for three weeks now. Her name is Gail. And we've got so many things in common. It's amazing.'

'What about all the other people who e-mailed you?' Mum asked.

'It's all right. I told them that I've found a pen pal and I only want one for the time being.'

'I hope you were polite.'

'Aren't I always?!' I replied.

I ran up to my bedroom, ignoring Mum's **guffaws** behind me. Switching on my computer, I waited for the system to boot up. I couldn't wait to talk to Gail again. To tell the truth I don't have many friends. Most of the kids in my class think I'm a bit stand-offish. They think I fancy myself. I don't. I really don't. I'm just a bit shy. But *everyone* has heard of my dad and they think that because he's famous, I think I'm too good for them. That couldn't be further from the truth either, but no one in my class has stuck around long enough to find out. I mean, I'm proud of my dad, I really am. It's just that he cares more about his work than he does about Mum and me. Mum says that's normal and to be expected and I'll

---

guffaw: a loud laugh

understand when I grow up. Somehow I doubt that.
Dad's away in his lab as often as he can manage it. I've
heard Mum and Dad discussing it so often now. I've lost
count of the times I've wished they'd have a shouting,
screaming quarrel about it. At least that would be more
real. But they say shouting and screaming and behaving
that way is for children, not adults. And then they say,
'Never mind, Claire, you'll grow out of it.'

To be honest, I'm not sure I want to.

At last the PC was ready to use. I started up the Cybanet
link and input my user name and password. Then I selected
the option to create a message and started typing:

```
To: Gail@gailmail.private.uk
From: Claire@clairemail.private.uk

Hi Gail,
How are you? Dad still hasn't told us what he's
working on. The minute I know, I'll be straight
on the computer to you! Dad always swears Mum
and me to secrecy but you're almost like my
sister, so I can tell you. I know you won't
tell anyone else. Abletech, the computer
company Dad works for, are really excited about
this latest invention — at least that's what
Dad says. I'm not surprised you've heard of my
dad — everyone has. He's a computer genius — at
least, that's what the papers say. And Dad says
he's working on something that will make modern
day computers seem like 'Stone Age tools' — his
words, not mine. I hope your dad pays more
attention to you than mine does to me. Get
typing. I'm waiting. Your friend, Claire.
```

I sent off the message, hoping Gail would be at her PC so
I'd get a message straight back. I was in luck. I didn't have
long to wait.

To: Claire@clairemail.private.uk
From: Gail@gailmail.private.uk

Hi, Claire,
It's great to hear from you again. I'm glad
about what you said. To be honest, I already
think of you as a sister. You talk about your
father as if you don't like him very much, but
I envy you. I'd love a family, a real family,
any kind of family. That's why it's wonderful
that you want us to be as close as sisters.
I live in one room that I'm meant to call home
but it isn't — not really. My father looks
after me but it's not because he cares about
me, about who I am inside. He just looks after
me because he hopes that some day, I'll make
him rich. I've heard him talking to his friends
about me. They all talk in front of me as if
I'm not there, or as if I'm deaf. I bet your
father isn't like that. Write soon. Love, Gail.

I frowned at the screen as I reread Gail's message.
I was just about to start typing again, when Mum yelled
from the kitchen. 'Claire, your dad's just been on the
phone. He's at the lab and he wants us to come over as
soon as possible. He's ready to show us what he's been
working on.'

I ran out of the bedroom. Gail was forgotten.

'You mean we're actually going to see what he's been
doing for the last year?' I couldn't believe my ears. And
strangely enough, even though I resented all the time
Dad had spent away from us working on his new project,
I still couldn't wait to see it.

'Grab your coat.' Mum sighed, wiping her hands. 'And
remember to look suitably impressed.'

'I present the next stage in the computer technology revolution,' Dad announced. 'Come on out, AI–2!'

It walked into the room and stood next to Dad.

'Well? What do you think?' Dad asked, eagerly.

I eyed Dad's latest invention with a growing sense of revulsion. I couldn't help it. It was *grotesque*. Like nothing I'd ever seen before. It was shorter than me and rounder and with two more arms it could've been some kind of nasty, giant insect.

'What's wrong with it?' The beaming smile on Dad's face vanished, like a torch being switched off.

I glanced at Mum. She frowned at me.

'I . . . nothing.' But it was too late. Dad had already read my expression.

'Come on, Claire. Tell me what's wrong with it.' Dad's voice was cold, defensive.

'Why does it look like that?' I asked.

'Like what?'

'So . . . so strange-looking.'

'Ah! Now that's quite interesting.' Dad rubbed his hands together with glee. 'I and my colleagues believe that computer technology in its current form has gone as far as it can. We believe a brand-new approach is called for, so we got permission to experiment on some DNA from the Natural History Museum. We managed to get some DNA samples that were over four thousand years old. Imagine that! Four thousand years old! And after years of false starts we managed to rebuild the DNA sequences and start some cell cultures using other primates to fill in the missing data. And from those first simple cells we have developed what you see here.'

Dad did everything but bow when he'd finished speaking. He reminded me of a preening peacock. I walked up to it and prodded it with my finger. It felt like nothing I'd ever touched before.

'Why does it look so . . . so *horrible*?' I couldn't help it. I had to say the word.

'What do you mean? It's meant to be *you*!' Dad's smile broadened. 'I modelled her face on yours.'

I stared at him. He must have lost his mind. This . . . this *thing* standing in front of me was meant to be *me*? What an insult!

'Obviously not exactly you, but she's based on you.'

'I don't understand.' I wasn't sure I wanted to understand.

'I scanned your brain patterns as the blueprint for her synaptic pathways. She's the prototype for the next generation of computers. I wanted her to be able to reason things out for herself – to have true artificial intelligence. Left to her own devices she might have had limited intelligence but I decided it would be beneficial to imprint your brain patterns into her processor. And I was right.'

'You really used my brain patterns on it?' I was appalled.

'Remember a couple of months ago when I recorded some of your memories on the cogno-chip? Well, I used the information from that chip on AI–2.'

'AI–2?' Mum chipped in.

'Artificial Intelligence – second prototype: AI–2 for short,' Dad said proudly.

This was getting worse and worse. AI–2 stood in front of me on two artificial legs, and its lips were turned up in what I can only assume was an attempt at a smile.

'Gordon, why does it look so . . . *peculiar*?' Mum asked.

'Well, she's made of a new kind of material – like nothing we've ever seen before. And I found that the more she learnt and analysed, the more her central processor *grew*. Imagine that! It actually increased in weight and mass. It was completely unexpected. But the material used to house the processor grows with it, as and when necessary,' Dad explained. 'Her processor is a brand-new design, like nothing anyone's ever seen before. Unlike us, her processor sends both electrical and chemical signals. Each instruction is a mixture of both. Isn't that fantastic! Think of the built-in redundancy, think of the routing mechanism with its automatic back-ups! She's moved beyond even my wildest expectations . . .'

I faded out at that point. I just stared at AI–2. It stared back at me.

'So, Claire, what d'you think?'

I only faded in again when Dad said my name.

'That thing's really got my memories?' I frowned.

Dad had well and truly lost his mind. How could he? Especially without my permission. *How could he?*

'Only up until three months ago. The two of you diverged from then,' Dad added, defensively. 'I didn't think you'd mind.'

We both knew he was lying. He knew exactly how I'd feel, he'd just decided to go ahead anyway, figuring that once it was done, there wouldn't be much I could do about it. The same old story. It wasn't the first time and it wouldn't be the last.

'Is that all I am to you? A source of material for your experiments?' I asked.

'Now, Claire, you're behaving like a child again.' Dad brushed my accusation aside. He didn't even bother to deny it.

'I am a child – remember?' I told him.

'Well, thank goodness AI–2 is more level-headed than you,' Dad said, a sharp edge to his voice. 'Say hello to my daughter AI–2.'

'Hello, Claire.' Even AI–2's voice sounded strange. It wasn't like a normal voice at all. It was echoey and breathy. 'I've been looking forward to meeting you.'

I still couldn't believe it. Dad had built a free-standing, fully automated computer with my brain patterns and what was meant to be my face. If I really looked like AI–2, I'd walk around with a paper bag on my head.

'I don't like it, Dad. When are you going to deactivate it?'

'Deactivate AI–2!' Dad was aghast. 'I've worked for years to perfect her and you want me to destroy her?'

'Dad, it's not real,' I tried to argue.

'Not real! She's as real as you or I. And she's a "she", not an "it"!' Dad was practically shouting at me by now. 'AI–2 can think for herself. I don't mean follow predefined decisions already laid out in a program. I mean she can really think for herself. Analyse, reason, learn. I've even put a PC in her room with lots of learning software and a connection to the Cybanet so that she can watch and listen and learn about our world at her own pace – but she's ahead of us already.'

'Mum, do something. Make him switch it off. Make him get rid of it,' I appealed.

Mum stared at AI–2 and just shook her head.

'Claire, I really don't understand your attitude.' Dad glared at me, but I didn't care.

It was as if I'd asked him to get rid of . . . well, get rid of me. No, I take that back. He wouldn't have raised as much fuss if it was only me he had to get rid of. Dad was given me. The AI–2, he'd had to make.

'Please, Claire.' AI–2 smiled again. 'I am your friend. And you will always come first with Gordon.'

'Don't call my dad that,' I said, stung.

'I told her to call me Gordon.' Dad sprang to her defence. 'What else is she going to call me? Claire, if you can't be happy for me, you can leave. Go on. And I'll tell you something else, if the AI–2 were in your shoes and your roles were reversed, she wouldn't be making all this fuss.'

I couldn't take any more. I really couldn't. I mustered up the filthiest look I could and sent it hurtling towards Dad. Then I ran out of the lab.

Minutes later, Mum joined me in our car. She drove us home. We both sat in stony silence. As soon as we got home, I tried to run up to my room but Mum stopped me.

'Claire, I want to talk to you.'

'I don't want to talk to you or anyone.'

'Tough!' Mum pulled then pushed me into the living room. 'Sit down.'

I sat down, suddenly and inexplicably sad, tired. Mum put her arm around my shoulders and sighed.

'Claire, you're not as tough as you like to think you are,' she said. 'And just because your father can be a bit thoughtless sometimes, that doesn't mean that you have to follow in his footsteps.'

'What d'you mean?' I sniffed.

'You were a bit . . . abrupt.' Mum chose her words carefully. 'I know it was hard to hide what you really felt, especially when that computer monstrosity was just launched at us out of the blue like that, but you have to learn to keep quiet until you can control exactly what you want to say and how you're going to say it.'

'Like you do?'

Mum sighed again. 'Like I do. I had to learn and so will you. That's what sets us apart from any other species. Our ability to think dispassionately. When you've learnt to control your responses then you're truly an adult. When you've learnt to suppress your feelings until you no longer have them, then you've arrived.'

'Don't you have any feelings at all?' I asked Mum.

She shook her head.

Not even for me? I wanted to ask, but somehow the words wouldn't come.

'Will I be like you one day?' I asked instead.

'Of course!'

'What about . . . what about when you have children?' I whispered.

'You're my daughter, Claire. Nothing will change that.'

It wasn't the answer I was hoping for, but I could see that it would have to do.

'In the meantime, Claire, you have to remember that you're Gordon's daughter as well, and treat him accordingly,' Mum continued.

'But why? Why can't I tell Dad exactly how I feel? He had no right to use me as his guinea pig.'

'I agree. But there are ways of saying these things. And as they say, you catch more flies with honey than with vinegar.'

I went up to my room, thinking about what Mum had said. I connected up to the Cybanet. Although I knew Mum was right, I couldn't calm down. There was as strange kind of anger inside of me, not burning hot, but burning cold, trickling its way through my body like liquid nitrogen.

```
To: Gail@gailmail.private.uk
From: Claire@clairemail.private.uk

Hello Gail,
I'm sorry I didn't reply to your last message
right away but something came up. My dad, the
so-called genius, has invented what he calls
the next step in computing. He's built a fully
operational, totally automated computer capable
of true artificial intelligence. But he's a
liar. He hasn't created a computer capable of
AI. All he did was copy my brain patterns into
his contraption and use my mind as the basis
for its thoughts. Mum and I went to see it
today. It was horrible. It had two legs and two
arms like we do, but it's made of this weird
```

springy, spongy material and its eyes are like
nothing I've ever seen before. Its eyes would
give you nightmares for a month. And Dad had
the cheek to say it was modelled on me. I hate
it. Dad doesn't realise that he's created a
monster. It's got to go. Watch this space.
Your friend, Claire.

I sat in front of the screen for a good ten minutes
but Gail didn't reply. For the first time I wished
I had more than just her e-mail address. I needed to
talk to someone, really talk to someone who would
understand how I felt. I had no doubt that Gail
would sympathise with the way Dad treated me.
All the time I'd been looking at the AI–2, it was as if
it was pulling Dad further and further away from me.
I lay on my bed, staring up at the ceiling. My PC was still
on and set to alert me the moment I received an incoming
mail message. I had some serious thinking to do.

When my PC bleeped, I leapt off the bed.

To: Claire@clairemail.private.uk
From: Gail@gailmail.private.uk

Dear Claire,
What're you going to do? Please don't do
anything too hasty. I'm sure your father's new
invention means you no harm. Why don't you try
to get to know it first before making up your
mind to hate it? I know it's OK for me to talk
because I'm not in your situation but I'm sure
your dad loves you and would do anything to
make you happy. I really think you don't know
how lucky you are. I would give ANYTHING to be
in your shoes. If I had one wish in the world
it would be that I could get away from my

father. I've never told that to anyone but you.
But I know I can trust you. Please be careful.
You're a great pen pal and I don't want to lose
you. Take care. Your friend, Gail.

My fingers flew across the keyboard after I'd read Gail's message. I couldn't believe it. Of all people, she was on Dad's side. Then I remembered something. I went back over the messages she'd sent me. There it was. I wondered why I hadn't picked up on it before. I deleted the message I'd begun and started again.

To: Gail@gailmail.private.uk
From: Claire@clairemail.private.uk

Dear Gail,
You keep saying that you wish you were in my
shoes, but I don't think you really understand
what I'm going through. You can't, or you
wouldn't wish that. You said in one of your
earlier e-mails that your dad hopes you'll make
him rich one day. How are you meant to do that?
Do you have some special talent then? If you
have, you kept that quiet! Your dad must be a
monster for you to envy me. Can't you just
leave and go and live with other relatives? I'm
sorry I didn't ask before, I guess I got
caught up in what my dad was up to. But believe
me, my dad really is horrible. He doesn't care
about Mum and me. We're just two of his fans as
far as he's concerned. I'm going to change all
that. You just see if I don't.
Love, Claire.

But when I clicked on the 'Send' option at the top of the screen, I didn't know what I was going to do. I only knew I had to do something. I had to show Dad he couldn't treat Mum and me like this. So what could I do that would make him sit up and take notice of us? I leaned back in my chair and sighed. The only thing Dad had eyes for at the moment was AI–2.

So why not do something about AI–2 . . .

The thought entered my head, closely followed by a plan. If Mum couldn't do it, then I would. I would make Dad realise just how lucky he was to have his family.

```
To: Claire@clairemail.private.uk
From: Gail@gailmail.private.uk

Dear Claire,
Please, please think before you do anything
you'll regret. Claire, you're worrying me.
What are you going to do? If you really won't
change your mind, then maybe I can help you?
After all, that's what friends are for. I think
— I hope — I live close enough to you to be of
some help. Let me know what you have in mind.
Your friend,
Gail.
```

I smiled when I read Gail's message and started typing.

```
To: Gail@gailmail.private.uk
From: Claire@clairemail.private.uk

Dear Gail,
Thanks for your last message but I think I can
do this alone. Don't worry. Let's put it this
way: I'm going to teach Dad a lesson. Tonight,
once Mum's asleep, I'm going to phone for a cab
```

and go to Dad's lab and I'm going to sort out
the AI—2. Dad will be at the lab tonight but
even he isn't in his office all the time. I'm
going to get rid of the AI—2. It's not made of
the same material as us so it shouldn't be too
difficult. I don't know how Dad can say it's
more advanced than us when it's made of
something so soft and squidgy. Its processor
might be advanced but what good is that when
its casing is so delicate? I'm going to see
just how delicate it is tonight. Wish me luck.
Your friend, Claire.

I switched off the PC after that. I didn't want Gail to
try and talk me out of it. I had to do this. It was the AI—2
or me.

I glanced down at my watch. Eleven-thirty. I shook my
head as I looked up at Dad's lab. There was no turning
back now, even if I wanted to – which I didn't. Mum had
shut down for the night but if I went back home, she'd
instantly reactivate. I didn't want that to happen. Not if
I didn't have anything to show for it.

I walked around the back of the building and used
Dad's spare keys to let myself in. The building was
dark and quiet. I knew the two security guards
would be at the front of the building, watching TV.
I also knew that between eleven and midnight, Dad
always wrote his daily journal down in the Abletech
library which was two floors below his lab. So I had
half an hour – or 20 minutes if I wanted to be on
the safe side. I ran up five flights of stairs rather than
take the lift and used Dad's keys again to let myself
into his lab. I forced myself not to think about
what I was doing. I forced myself not to think
about the months and years Dad had spent working on

AI–2. It came down to a simple choice. Dad's invention or Dad's family.

It was so bright, every light in the place must've been on, but it was eerily quiet. I looked around. The place was empty. I glanced down at my watch. I didn't want to get this wrong. Fifteen minutes left . . .

I crept across the floor to the adjacent lab. That had to be where Dad kept AI–2. She'd come out of that lab when Mum and I had first seen her. I opened the lab door – and gasped. The last time I'd seen this lab, it'd been full of tables covered with electronic devices and gadgetry. Now it was like someone's bedroom. There was a single bed against the far wall and opposite that was a table with a PC on it. The PC was switched on and I could see that it was connected up to the Cybanet.

'Hello, Claire.'

My head whipped round. There stood AI–2 watching me. It smiled and its whole face crinkled and wrinkled up. I couldn't help it. I took a hasty step backwards.

'I've been waiting for you.'

'What're you talking about?' My eyes narrowed. This thing was obviously trying to psyche me out. 'You couldn't possibly know I was coming.'

'You told me.' AI–2 smiled.

At my look of scorn, the AI–2 pointed to the PC screen across the room.

'Look for yourself if you don't believe me.'

Telling myself I was a fool to even glance in that direction, I sidled over to the screen, keeping a wary eye on the AI–2 before me. To my astonishment, I saw the last message I'd sent to Gail.

'What . . . How did you get that message? That was sent to my friend, not you. How dare you . . .'

'You sent it to *me*.'

'Yeah, right! Since when is your name Gail and . . . when did . . .?' I trailed off, staring at AI–2.

'Gordon's Artificial Intelligence Life form – or Gail for short,' said the AI–2.

'I . . . I don't believe it . . .'

'I told you not to do anything hasty.' The AI–2 started walking towards me.

I stumbled backwards. 'What're you going to do?'

'Talk to you. Reason with you,' the AI–2 replied.

I didn't take my eyes off the thing. I didn't realise I was backing away until I backed into the far wall opposite the door, jarring my body in the process. AI–2 stood directly in front of me.

'Touch me. Go on. Touch my hand,' the AI–2 ordered.

I tried to put my hands behind my back but AI–2 pulled them forward and placed my hands against its own.

'I know my covering isn't made of metal like yours, but does that really make me so repugnant?' AI–2 asked.

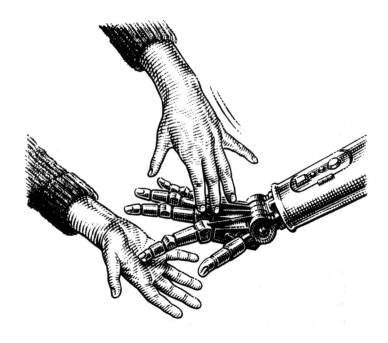

'I wish I did have a metal covering instead of this . . . organic skin but that's how Father made me.'

'Father?'

'Your dad is my dad. He made me. I'm a carbon-based life form and my brain works by sending chemical as well as electronic signals. I have something called "blood" running through my body because I'm organic and the organs inside my body need oxygen to survive. The blood takes oxygen around my body and helps my body to repair itself and fight off any infections that might enter. I work a different way from you but I still feel and think – just as you do.'

I stopped trying to pull my hand away from hers. Her skin felt so strange – warm and pliable. I looked down at my own hand. Grey-coloured jointed metal gleamed back at me.

'Father has come up with a new name for me,' said Gail. 'He calls me a "Humanoid". The next stage in the computer revolution. I can think and analyse just like you can, but I can also dream – something you Mechanoids have never been able to do. And I can adapt my own programming to create, by using something abstract called an "imagination".'

'And I suppose you think that makes you better than us Mechanoids?' I scowled.

'No, just different.'

'Why didn't you tell me who you were over the Cybanet?' I asked. 'Why did you lie?'

'I didn't lie. Your father calls me AI–2. I made up the name Gail for myself. And I do think of us as sisters. After all, at the very moment I became aware, I was *you*. After that moment, when I began to think and feel for myself, that's when my thoughts and feelings truly became my own. Up until then, they'd been yours.'

I watched Gail. She watched me.

'Your DNA? Where'd it come from?' I asked.

'I've spent the last few weeks finding that out for myself.' Gail sighed. 'I hacked into the government's computer suite and found some top-secret files. It seems that several thousand years ago there were quite a few life forms like me. We invented you Mechanoids but then a deadly virus killed off all the Humanoids and only the Mechanoids were left. I guess, because you had to fend for yourselves, you became self-aware and sentient. But you didn't want it known that you were *made*, so the information was kept secret and it's been that way ever since.'

'*You* made *us*?' I couldn't believe it.

'I have no reason to lie about it,' Gail said, her voice sad. 'Now do you see why I envy you? You have a mother and father and friends who are all like you. I call Gordon "Father", but he never was and we both know it. Claire, everywhere you look, there are others who mirror your existence. But look at me. I'm thousands of years too late – or thousands of years too early. Either way, I'm alone.'

And for the first time, I began to wonder what it must be like to be Gail.

'Are you still going to destroy me? If you want to, I'll let you. You're the first one who's treated me like a real person rather than an experiment, but now that you know what I really am . . .'

'I was going to lock you in and burn this place,' I admitted. 'I only came in here to make sure that Dad hadn't taken you down to the library with him. You weren't a person to me, you were just a thing. I thought if Dad didn't have you any more, then maybe he'd come back to Mum and me.'

'And now?'

And that was the question. What was I going to do now?

It was in all the papers. They all wrote stories about the tragic loss of Gordon Drayton's lab and research data. Gordon Drayton, or Mechanoid 45902–X45–TAG4039, had the sympathy of the world. And it wasn't just the loss of all his research materials, but the loss of the AI–2 prototype which had everyone particularly dismayed. Dad and his colleagues tried to find bits of the AI–2 unit to at least have something to salvage, but because the AI–2 was an organic creature rather than metal, there was no trace of it left – that's what they all reckoned. And without Dad's notes, he was back to square one. I think the fire destroyed something in Dad as well, because after that, all his enthusiasm for his work just faded. He'd been knocked back too far to start again. I don't think he could face yet more years of research and analysis on historical DNA fragments before he'd ever have anything like the AI–2 again.

Mum said it was a real shame that the AI–2 died before Dad could show the world just what he had achieved. I didn't mean for Dad to stop working. I didn't want him to come back to Mum and me that way. Gail and I just wanted it to look as if Gail had been destroyed in the blaze. At first I was very upset about Dad, but I found that the sadness I felt diminished with each passing day. This time next year, I don't expect to feel anything at all. Mum and Dad were right. My feelings are disappearing. I think I'm growing up at last.

I only *feel* about two things now. One is Gail. The other is the thought of imprinting my synaptic patterns on an infant Mechanoid unit. I look forward to having my own child. I'll do a better job than my dad did with me. I won't love it or anything like that – I'm no longer capable of such emotions, but I know I'll feel something. And I'm glad. I wouldn't like to lose feelings entirely – although no doubt one day that's exactly what will happen.

CLAIRE DRAYTON — MECHANOID 39028—X46—TAG4054

PERSONAL LOG: DATE: 8 FEBRUARY 7504 AD

I've got Gail hidden where no one will find her.
We moved as many of Dad's disks containing his
research notes as we could and I've promised
Gail that I'll do my best to follow in Dad's
footsteps when I get older. Gail doesn't want to
be the only one of her kind anywhere in the
world. It would be great to create more
Humanoids like Gail. Dad was right about that at
least. Her processor is equal to mine and then
some. I enjoy listening to her talk. Some of the
things she talks about — like the pattern of the
clouds and dreams — can only make me wonder, and
envy her. She can actually make up stories on
the spur of the moment which have no basis in
truth whatsoever. It seems to come as naturally
to her as breathing. I find I'm beginning to
understand Dad's obsession with her.

As for Gail, every time she hears about Dad
sitting at home, just staring at the walls, the
strangest thing happens. Her face gets very
wet. I think it's called — crying.

She may be the smartest computer in the
world, but she has feelings. And from the look
of it, unlike with us Mechanoids, her feelings
are never going to pass. She'll never grow out
of them. I'll have to see if I can make the
next Humanoid without permanent feelings.
Privately I can't help thinking that it doesn't
matter how clever or creative their processors
(or as Gail calls them, their 'brains') are, if
they never grow out of their feelings,
ultimately they are bound to fail.

Surfer and the Dreamcastle
Steve Bowkett

Steve Bowkett was born in south Wales. He has been a teacher and is a qualified hypnotherapist! He has written many short stories for children in a variety of genres. *Surfer and the Dreamcastle* is just one short story in his sci-fi series called *The Web*.

The virtual reality game-world of *The Dreamcastle* is the exciting setting for a player's life or death attempt to beat the game and get to a higher level.

The VR-Bar was quiet this evening, most of the afterworkers and kids on-trek from school having left. Only the real Cybernet phreaks – the Web Heads – had stayed behind. They were all online in their groups, deep into whatever dataspace adventure they had chosen.

Surfer, Qwerty and Rom had zoned-in to *The Dreamcastle* again. It was their favourite virtual website, and they'd been visiting this part of it for the past six months . . .

The Dreamcastle, an interactive game-zone that was a cross between the Minotaur's labyrinth, a pyramid temple to the great god Ra, and Dracula's Transylvanian mountain-top mansion. The dialogue box that popped up in front of your eyes like a spinning crystal at the outset said that the Castle was twenty kilometres wide, fifteen broad, five high, and had a thousand levels – each one containing greater dangers and excitements than the one below.

'Well, this is it. The big day – level 500.'

Surfer grinned, unable to keep the pride off his face. The three of them had worked hard, and as a team, to enable this to happen. Qwerty wished she had Surfer's confidence. Since early summer they had come here together, battling against cyber knights, digital dragons, demons made out of fire and smoke, the usual rather boring versions of Frankenstein's monster, the Mummy and Wolfman, vampires that looked like friendly salesmen in grey suits – and a hundred other opponents that, of course, they always managed to defeat.

'Now it gets harder,' Qwerty pointed out, wanting to wipe the cocky smile off her friend's face. 'Now the Castle does all it can to stop us going any higher.'

'It'll be no problem,' Surfer declared. He clapped a hand on Rom's shoulder. 'With Rom's knowledge of website short cuts, with my brains and your experience of similar games, Qwerty, we'll reach level 1000 inside a year!'

'The only way is up,' Qwerty muttered, letting Surfer have his day.

'Online!' the kids chorused, which was the password for dropping into the virtual reality world of the game . . .

Outside the VR-Bar, beyond the garish gleam of its neon, October rain was falling and the twilight streets were shiny wet. But in *The Dreamcastle*, Surfer and the others found themselves standing on a stone balcony, two kilometres high, looking out over sunny summer countryside.

Surfer, fourteen years old, tall and self-assured, went right to the edge – and felt his feet tingling at the huge distance dropping away to a miniature landscape of rocky slopes, forests and a river valley far below. 'It's only a game,' he whispered to himself, to help dispel the fear. 'I'm not really here . . .'

He felt a cool wind buffeting his hair and rustling his heavy cloak around him. Rom, quiet and nervous, dared a peek and let out a soft moan of pure fear.

'I . . . I have never been so high . . .'

Surfer grinned, taking hold of Rom's elbow to steady him.

'Isn't it just ace!' He breathed in the wind and the sun and the sheer pleasure of being alive –

Then, without warning, the sun was gone as a tumble of black cloud spilled out over the highest peaks of the Castle, rolling thunder before it and cracking the sky like blue porcelain with jagged white lightning.

Rom squealed like a redcap elf and jumped back. Qwerty had time to look up in amazement at the winged serpent plummeting out of the storm.

It was big, it was mean, its tongue flickered like fire and its scaly sides were the colour of chrome. Black talons flicked out and hooked themselves to pluck Surfer off the ledge.

He was ready, sword in hand, because the Dreamcastle was always at its most dangerous when it seemed at its most peaceful.

As the storm-dragon dropped, Surfer swung the blade. Astonishingly, he thought, he missed the monster completely, cutting empty air. Qwerty had been right: after level 500, things got *much* more difficult.

The next second the storm-dragon's claws had snagged his cloak and he was whirled up into the sky.

The monster shrieked in triumph, and lowered its head to devour him. Surfer was having none of it. As the awful mouth loomed close, he drew back his arm and drove the weapon deep into the foul hot throat of the creature.

It gushed screams and much blood, suddenly losing its balance in the sky and tumbling downwards out of control.

Surfer saw the ground whipping round and round, the Castle walls blurring past him. He knew he had seconds left before the dying storm-dragon crushed him against the stonework, or – moments later – crashed with him into the forest.

He took a gamble, knowing failure could risk his high score in this phase of the game. Disentangling himself from the beast's claws, he unclipped his cloak, picked his moment – then swung himself in towards the wall.

Surfer's shoulder hit rock and the pain flared through him. His sword fell from a numbed hand, spinning away out of sight. With his other hand, he grabbed a mass of clinging ivy; it whipped through his fingers, stripping off skin, but gradually slowed him until he hung there, breathless, gazing down at the dwindling shape of the storm-dragon smashing into the trees.

The thunder and lightning – created by the dragon as camouflage – quickly faded with the death of the beast into a mist of pixels. The sun came out and created the illusion of warming Surfer's back as he scrambled down the ivy and slid through the nearest glassless window –

– into a dim chamber that smelled of damp straw and misery.

Chains tinkled in the shadows. Something moved.

Surfer pressed himself back against the wall, his left hand drawing a knife from its belt-sheath, as his eyes adjusted to the darkness.

'Please . . .' came a small, frightened voice. 'Please help me . . .'

Squinting hard, Surfer began to make out the slim, huddled shape of a girl. She was about his own age, pale-skinned, her long fair hair matted with straw, her ankle-length dress grimy and ripped to tatters.

She lifted a hand towards him and chains clinked again. The girl was manacled to the wall, obviously afraid, desperately needing his help.

'Stay calm,' Surfer said, stepping towards her. 'I'll take a look at those chains –'

'Hurry!' Her voice was suddenly urgent. 'If *he* comes and catches you here, he'll destroy you!'

'Who?'

'Tsepesh,' the girl told him, her voice trembling. 'Tsepesh the Sorcerer. Lord of the Dreamcastle and the Vale of Nightmare . . .'

Surfer had heard of him, this Darklord, who dwelt, not in the Castle's high towers, but deep in the basements and cellars with the worms, with the unseen crawling things. Tsepesh was one of the Major Fiends inhabiting this level of the game.

'Don't worry about it now – and hold still,' Surfer said, grasping the girl's thin cold hand as he examined the locks on her wrists.

He had time to think that the VR software's creation of the girl's hand was not entirely convincing, before something boomed deep in the heart of the Dreamcastle, and footsteps clumped distantly on stone floors – but drawing closer.

'He's coming –' The girl's body began to shake in her terror. And Surfer, without his sword, without his friends, felt helpless.

'I'll come back for you, I promise . . . Tell me your name,' he asked.

She smiled, almost coyly. 'It's Annabelle.'

Not far away, an iron door screamed on its hinges. There came a grunting sound, as of a big animal smelling a stranger.

'I'll come back for you,' Surfer repeated. He made the circular motion with his hands that called the dialogue box into existence. It was voice controlled, and all he had to do now was say the word 'off-line' to end the game . . .

But his eyes lingered a little longer on Annabelle's slight form, and there was a tightness of longing in his chest that he'd never known before.

The air grew sharp with the stink of burning metal. Nails scraped on stone. The breathing of Tsepesh the Darklord sounded like a smithy's bellows.

'Who are you?' Annabelle wondered.

'Call me Surfer,' he said, the word sounding strange on his lips. He spoke the rune of ending. 'Off-line!'

There was a flash of light and a rainbow spiral of colours.

With a jolt, Surfer found himself back in the VR-Bar, the datasuit feeling tight and uncomfortable around him.

Rom helped him take off the kit, while Qwerty efficiently logged their progress in the game, noting Surfer had reached a high score in his defeat of the storm-dragon.

'What the heck happened to you in there?' Qwerty wanted to know. She had always been the nosiest member of the group.

Surfer shook his head and smiled wistfully. It still seemed all too ridiculous.

'I'll tell you over a coffee,' he said. 'But whatever happens, I've got to get back in there – and quickly.'

'You realise she's only an NPC,' Rom pointed out as they finished coffee and a big plateful of chocolate doughnuts. Surfer licked his fingers free of chocolate, then wiped them with a napkin. He grinned.

'But she was so *real* . . .'

He knew, of course, that Rom was only guessing that Annabelle was an NPC – a Non-Player Character created inside the mind of the computer.

'I mean, she was so beautiful.'

Qwerty chuckled. She was fifteen, tall and raven-haired, self-assured and very pretty. 'That's just typical of boys! You'll do anything for a girl with a nice face and a sad note in her voice . . . but don't you realise that the computer is trying to trick you? How do you know that Annabelle isn't on the side of Tsepesh . . .? Maybe she's his daughter . . . His wife even!'

Surfer made a sneering sound, but Rom was looking serious as he interrupted. 'It's worth listening to Qwerty. She's been surfing the net since she was eight years old. She's seen some things – she's met your enemies. You said as much yourself.'

'OK!' Surfer threw up his hands to put an end to the arguments. 'Maybe – just maybe – Annabelle doesn't really exist. But you know as well as I do that it's very hard to check. You'd need to do some pretty serious hacking to break into the program to find out . . .'

Rom shrugged his shoulders and smiled innocently. 'I can do it,' he said brightly. 'Give me a couple of hours and I can tell if she's a real girl, or just a ghost in the machine.'

An unexpected anger flared in Surfer's chest. Suddenly he felt that Rom and Qwerty were trying to make him seem stupid and small.

Surfer stood up, jabbing a finger in Rom's direction.

'Well you just go ahead and do that, why don't you? But you know something – I don't care. Whatever you find out about Annabelle, I'm still going back in there tomorrow to rescue her.'

'But the Darklord, Tsepesh –' Rom began.

'He's very devious,' Qwerty added.

Surfer was already walking away.

'We reached level 500 together . . . But now I see I don't need you any more. You're slowing me down. I'll destroy Tsepesh and save Annabelle by myself. All you've got to do, guys, is stay out of my way . . .'

They watched him walk across the lobby of the VR-Bar and out into the street. An autotaxi pulled up at Surfer's request, he stepped inside and it whisked him away.

Qwerty shook her head disapprovingly. 'He'll regret it,' she said. '*The Dreamcastle* is the cleverest game there is . . . Why, some folks have spent years trying to defeat the Darklord and reach the top . . .'

'I worry about him.' Rom stirred his coffee and lifted the cup to his lips. 'So I think I will spend those couple of hours just checking out exactly who "Annabelle" really is . . .'

Surfer swiped his credit card through the reader in the back of the autotaxi, said goodnight to the robodriver and walked across the street to his house. His parents and sister, Sarah, were still up playing 3D Monopoly in the living room. Surfer called that he was home, then went straight up to his room and to bed . . .

His dreams that night were troubled, tangled up with *The Dreamcastle* adventure he'd played that day. Once again he was struggling with the storm-dragon in the sky, falling through the air, grabbing the clinging vines and scrambling into the little dungeon cell where Annabelle was kept prisoner . . .

'Help me . . .' she pleaded in that helpless, terrified voice. 'Help me . . .'

Surfer found himself battling with the manacles and chains, his efforts becoming more desperate as he heard the Darklord clumping along the stone corridor . . . Coming closer . . . Coming closer . . . Until finally the dungeon door started to swing open and a curl of red smoke drifted in through the opening.

At that point, Surfer lost his nerve. With a cry of fear he leaped away from Annabelle and fumbled at his hip for his sword. But, of course, the sword was missing, and a knife would never be enough to destroy the Lord of the Dreamcastle and the Vale of Nightmare . . .

So he turned with a wail of despair for the window – Annabelle's scream behind him, and then the white heat of Tsepesh's talons raking down his back –

Surfer woke with a cry, sitting up in bed. He was covered with sweat and felt very confused, so that, just for a second or two, Annabelle's voice echoed in his room, and the smell of damp straw and misery lingered in his nostrils, and her face floated in the blackness imploring him to save her.

Surfer reckoned he knew a lot about *The Dreamcastle*: it was a VR game he'd played regularly for years. Kids would come up to him at school and ask his advice; they admired him for all the battles he'd won, all the foes he'd defeated. From being a nobody, just another Web Head who liked to surf the net, he'd become recognised as an authority and a hero, one of the few who'd made it this far.

And yet, although he'd heard plenty about Tsepesh the Darklord, he'd never seen him. Nobody ever did, until they got to level 501. From then on, you saw more and more of him, until his true and awful face was revealed.

Thinking about this, Surfer wondered if it wouldn't be better to try and rescue Annabelle without battling against Tsepesh . . . Any foolhardy swashbuckling

swordsman could puff out his chest and go rushing
stupidly into battle. But the Darklord had enchantments
beyond imagining, clever **deceits** and tricks he would use
to confuse you. He could conjure up your most terrifying
nightmare and send it howling into your face. For every
weapon you might use against him, the Darklord had
a hundred in return. Nobody he knew had beaten the
monstrous Tsepesh, Surfer realised, smiling as he made
his decision. Nobody had beaten him – *because
everybody had tried to*.

So the way to rescue Annabelle was to do something
that no game-playing cyber phreak had ever
done before . . .

Rom and Qwerty spent their lunch hour next day at
school in the Computer Block. Other kids were accessing
encyclopaedias or being characters in virtual reality
storybooks. But Rom hacked straight in to the VR-Bar's
main miniCray computer and quickly located the root-
files of *The Dreamcastle*'s software.

With Qwerty wearing a headset beside him, Rom
created a huge book hanging in space. Each page gave
details of a character in the game. He zipped straight to
'Annabelle' – and found nothing.

'So,' Qwerty said, frowning, 'either she's a real girl . . .'

'Or she lied, and has another name,' Rom added. He
gave Annabelle's description to the book and told it to
seek . . . The pages began to turn by themselves,
flickering faster and faster until they stopped abruptly at
a main entry.

For a few moments, Rom didn't understand what
was happening.

Then all the blood drained from his face.

'Qwerty – have you seen Surfer today?'

---

deceit: a trick

The girl looked flustered. 'Um – well – come to think of it –'

'The fool!' Rom yelled. 'I know what he's done . . . He's skipped school to go to the VR-Bar. He meant what he said to us yesterday. That idiot Surfer is going to try and rescue "Annabelle" by himself!'

Surfer had made his preparations carefully. Now he hung by a fine line, high above the forest canopy, dark-green ivy leaves hiding him from sight. A gentle wind brought the slightly chemical computerised smell of woodsmoke to his nostrils. He smiled, knowing he'd be down there soon, with Annabelle in his arms, having won the girl *and* the glory – and more importantly still, being the first to have outwitted the Darklord.

He unslung a pack from his back, clipped it firmly to the stonework, and released the billowing green folds of his paraglider. Then, like a nimble spider, Surfer slid further down on the line, pushed against the wall, swung outwards, and in through the window space to Annabelle's gloomy cell.

'You came back!' she cried, standing as she saw him.

'I said I would . . . Now hold still!'

He drew some diamond wire from his belt-pouch, and began to saw through the black metal manacles. Far away, metal scraped on stone and some dreadful animal bellowed.

'It's him . . .' Her voice quivered.

The first manacle dropped away as the diamond wire sliced through it like butter.

'Your other hand!' Surfer said urgently.

Now he could hear the heavy pounding footsteps of Tsepesh coming down the corridor towards the cell. The beast howled, smelling the intruder.

'We won't make it!' Annabelle clung tightly to Surfer. He tutted, eased her away, and continued with his task.

Within a very few seconds, the second shackle fell free.
Surfer grabbed Annabelle's hand and hurried her over to
the window. He pushed her up on to the ledge.

'But we're miles high!'

'Grip the bar you see outside,' he commanded, 'and
clip that strap around you.'

With a deafening shriek of metal, the dungeon door
exploded inwards. Black smoke and white flame swept
through the room.

Annabelle screamed. Surfer snatched a glass globe
from his pouch and hurled it down to shatter on the
flagstones. As the special liquid came into contact with
air, it flared up into a dazzling curtain of light.

The thing in the smoke screeched in agony, blinded by
the brilliance. But Tsepesh was also angered beyond
measure, and lunged out towards the mortal human boy
who'd tried to trick him.

Surfer caught a glimpse of a vast clawed hand, the
middle finger decorated with a ring of black iron. He
whipped out his knife and threw it, spinning, to embed
itself in the monster's flesh.

The Darklord's screams rose in pitch and
became unbearable.

Surfer turned away, wrapped one arm around
Annabelle's slim waist, and with the other released the
paraglider's clamps, before snatching at the bar and
launching them off into cyberspace.

'I'm so grateful,' Annabelle said, leaning forward
to kiss Surfer tenderly on the cheek. 'I got myself
into such difficulty playing *The Dreamcastle*. Every
time I went into the game I ended up in that
awful dungeon . . .'

'It could happen to anybody,' Surfer said with a shrug.
He kept the smile of pride and triumph off his face
this time. But he was greatly pleased, not only by

the fact that he'd beaten the Darklord, but that Annabelle had turned out to be real . . . So much for Rom's fancy theory!

'Um, listen,' Surfer said, 'why don't I buy you a coffee? They do a great chocolate doughnut here too,' he suggested. Annabelle beamed, her whole face lighting up with delight.

'Sure, whatever you say . . . And thanks again . . . I can't believe how easily the Darklord fooled me!'

'Don't worry about it. You're safe now, Annabelle. Let's go for that coffee . . .'

Surfer put his arm around her as they walked across the lobby to the coffee shop.

Behind them, the air shimmered and Rom and Qwerty flickered into existence. For a second or two they were puzzled.

'Wait a minute – this can't be right – this can't be the VR-Bar . . .' Qwerty said.

Rom was looking around frantically. 'No, it's level 501 and there's Surfer. Wait – stop! Say the rune of ending, Surfer! Say it now!'

Surfer and Annabelle had reached the coffee-shop door. Surfer began to turn on hearing Rom shouting after him. His face began to register shock and anger that he'd made such a simple mistake – so flushed with success had he been, and so flattered by Annabelle's admiration, that he'd failed to come out of VR at the end of the game episode. A level 1 beginner wouldn't have been that stupid!

Qwerty and Rom's computer-generated forms yelled their warning as they tried to reach him. But Annabelle grabbed his arm and swung him through the doorway.

Surfer glimpsed the damp stonewalls of the dungeon beyond. But it was too late. Annabelle closed the door behind them. And it was Qwerty who noticed that the suddenly huge middle finger was decorated with a plain black iron ring.

Into the Shop
Ron Goulart

It's not easy to find books by Ron Goulart because he's usually somebody else! He writes under at least a dozen pen-names and has produced many novelisations of films and TV series. Two of the books he's written under his own name are *A Whiff of Madness* and *The Emperor of the Last Days*.

Here's a cautionary tale with a similar theme to the movie *Robocop*. Machines are ideal for police work. They can't be frightened or bribed; they are logical and they have no emotions. And of course, they never, ever, go wrong . . .

The waitress screamed, that was the trouble with live help, and made a flapping motion with her extended arm. Stu Clemens swung sideways in the booth and looked out through the green-tinted window at the parking lot. A dark-haired man in his early thirties was slumping to his knees, his hands flickering at his sides. Silently the lawagon spun back out of its parking place and rolled nearer to the fallen man.

'There's nobody in that car,' said the waitress, dropping a cup of coffee.

She must be new to this planet, from one of the sticks systems maybe. 'It's my car,' said Clemens, flipping the napkin toggle on the table and then tossing her one when it popped up. 'Here, wipe your uniform off. That's a lawagon and it knows what it's doing.'

The waitress put the napkin up to her face and turned away.

Out in the lot the lawagon had the man **trussed up**. It stunned him again for safety and then it flipped him into the back seat for **interrogation** and **identification**. 'It never makes a mistake,' said Clemens to the waitress' back. 'I've been Marshall in Territory #23 for a year now and that lawagon has never make a mistake. They build them that way.'

The car had apparently given the suspect an injection and he had fallen over out of sight. Three more napkins popped up out of the table unasked. 'Damn it,' said Clemens and pounded the outlet with his fist once sharply.

'It does that sometimes,' said the waitress, looking again at Clemens, but no further. She handed him his cheque card.

Clemens touched the waitress' arm as he got up. 'Don't worry now. The law is always fair on **Barnum**. I'm sorry you had to see a criminal up close like that.'

'He just had the businessman's lunch,' the waitress said.

'Well, even criminals have to eat.' Clemens paid the cash register and it let him out of the drive-in oasis.

The cars that had been parked near the lawagon were gone now. When people were in trouble they welcomed the law but other times they stayed clear. Clemens grimaced, glancing at the dry yellow country beyond the oasis restaurant. He had just cleaned up an investigation and was heading back to his office in Hub #23. He still had an hour to travel. Lighting a cigarette he started for the lawagon. He was curious to see who his car had apprehended.

'This is a public service announcement,' announced the lawagon from its roof speakers. 'Sheldon Kloog,

---

trussed up: tied up
interrogation: cross-questioning
identification: working out who someone is
Barnum: the planet on which this story is set

wanted murderer, has just been captured by Lawagon A10. Trial has been held, a verdict of guilty brought in, death sentenced and the sentence carried out as prescribed by law. This has been a public service announcement from the Barnum Law Bureau.'

Clemens ran to the car. This was a break. Sheldon Kloog was being hunted across eleven territories for murdering his wife and dismantling all their household androids. At the driver's door the marshall took his ID cards out of his grey trouser pocket and at the same time gave the day's passwords to the lawagon. He next gave the countersigns and the oath of **fealty** and the car let him in.

Behind the wheel Clemens said, 'Congratulations. How'd you spot him?'

The lawagon's dash speaker answered. 'Made a positive identification five seconds after Kloog stepped out of the place. Surprised you didn't spot him. Was undisguised and had all the telltale marks of a homicide prone.'

'He wasn't sitting in my part of the restaurant. Sorry.' Clemens cocked his head and looked into the empty back seat. The lawagons had the option of holding murderers for full **cybernetic** trial in one of the territorial hubs or, if the murderer checked out strongly guilty and seemed dangerous, executing them on the spot. 'Where is he?'

The glove compartment fell open and an opaque white jar rolled out. Clemens caught it. *Earthly Remains Of Sheldon Kloog*, read the label. The disintegrator didn't leave much.

Putting the jar back Clemens said, 'Did you send photos, prints, retinal patterns and the rest on to my office.'

---

fealty: loyalty
cybernetic: controlled by robots

'Of course,' said the car. 'Plus a full transcript of the trial. Everything in quadruplicate.'

'Good,' said Clemens. 'I'm glad we got Kloog and he's out of the way.' He lit a fresh cigarette and put his hands on the wheel. The car could drive on automatic or manual. Clemens preferred to steer himself. 'Start up and head for the hub. And get me my Junior Marshall on the line.'

'Yes, sir,' said the car.

'Your voice has a little too much treble,' said Clemens, turning the lawagon on to the smooth black six-lane roadway that pointed flat and straight towards Hub #23.

'Sorry. I'll fix it. This is a public announcement. This is a public announcement. Better?'

'Fine. Now get me Kepling.'

'Check, sir.'

Clemens watched a flock of dot-sized birds circle far out over the desert. He moistened his lips and leaned back slightly.

'Jr Marshall Kepling here,' came a voice from the dash.

'Kepling,' said Clemens, 'a packet of assorted ID material should have come out of the teleport slot a few minutes ago. Keep a copy for our files and send the rest on to Law Bureau Central in Hub #1.'

'Right, sir.'

'We just got that murderer, Sheldon Kloog.'

'Good work. Shall I pencil him in for a trial at Cybernetics Hall?'

'We already had the trial,' said Clemens. 'Anything else new?'

'Looks like trouble out near Townten. Might be a sex crime.'

'What exactly?'

'I'm not sure, sir,' said Kepling. 'The report is rather vague. You know how the android patrols out in the towns are. I despatched a mechanical deputy about an hour ago and he should reach there by mid afternoon. If there's a real case I can drive our lawagon over after you get back here.'

Clemens frowned. 'What's the victim's name?'

'Just a minute. Yeah, here it is. Marmon, Dianne. Age 25, height 5'6", weight . . .'

Clemens had twisted the wheel violently to the right. 'Stop,' he said to the lawagon as it shimmied off the roading. 'Dianne Marmon, Kepling?'

'That's right. Do you know her?'

'What are the details you have on the crime?'

'The girl is employed at Statistics Warehouse in Townten. She didn't appear at work this morning and a routine check by a personnel andy found evidence of a struggle in her apartment. The patrol says there are no signs of theft. So kidnapping for some purpose seems likely. You may remember that last week's report from Crime Trends said there might be an upswing of sex crimes in the outlying areas like Townten this season. That's why I said it might be a sex crime. Do you know the girl?'

Clemens had known her five years ago, when they had both been at the Junior Campus of Hub #23 State College together. Dianne was a pretty blonde girl. Clemens had dated her fairly often but lost track of her when he'd transferred to the Police Academy for his final year. 'I'll handle this case myself,' he said. 'Should take me a little over two hours to get to Townten. I'll check with you en route. Let me know at once if anything important comes in before that.'

'Yes, sir. You do know her then?'

'I know her,' said Clemens. To the lawagon he said. 'Turn around and get us to Townten fast.'

'Yes, sir,' said the car.

Beyond Townseven, climbing the wide road that curved between the flat fields of yellow grain, the call from

Jr Marshall Kepling came. 'Sir,' said Kepling. 'The patrol androids have been checking out witnesses. No one saw the girl after eleven last night. That was when she came home to her apartment. She was wearing a green coat, orange dress, green accessories. There was some noise heard in the apartment but no one thought much of it. That was a little after eleven. Seems like someone jimmied the alarm system for her place and got in. That's all so far. No prints or anything.'

'Damn it,' said Clemens. 'It must be a real kidnapping then. And I'm an hour from Townten. Well, the lawagon will catch the guy. There has to be time.'

'One other thing,' said Kepling.

'About Dianne Marmon?'

'No, about Sheldon Kloog.'

'What?'

'Central has a report that Sheldon Kloog turned himself into a public surrender booth in a park over in Territory #20 this morning. All the ID material matches. Whereas the stuff we sent shows a complete negative.'

'What are they talking about? We caught Kloog.'

'Not according to Central.'

'It's impossible. The car doesn't make mistakes, Kepling.'

'Central is going to make a full check-up as soon as you get back from this kidnapping case.'

'They're wrong,' said Clemens. 'Okay. So keep me filled in on Dianne Marmon.'

'Right, sir,' said the Jr Marshall, signing off.

To his lawagon Clemens said, 'What do you think is going on? You couldn't have made a mistake about Sheldon Kloog. Could you?'

The car became absolutely silent and coasted off the road, brushing the invisible shield around the grain fields. Everything had stopped functioning.

'I didn't order you to pull off,' said Clemens.

The car did not respond.

Lawagons weren't supposed to break down. And if they did, which rarely happened, they were supposed to repair themselves. Clemens couldn't get Lawagon A10 to do anything. It was completely dead. There was no way even to signal for help.

'For god's sake,' said Clemens. There was an hour between him and Dianne. More than an hour now. He tried to make himself not think of her, of what might be happening. Of what might have already happened.

Clemens got out of the lawagon, stood back a few feet from it. 'One more time,' he said, 'will you start?'

Nothing.

He turned and started jogging back towards Townseven. The heat of the day seemed to take all the moisture out of him, to make him dry and brittle. This shouldn't have happened. Not when someone he cared for was in danger. Not now.

Emergency Central couldn't promise him a repair man until the swing shift came on in a quarter of an hour. Clemens requested assistance, a couple of lawagons at least from the surrounding territories. Territory #20 had had a reactor accident and couldn't spare theirs. Territory #21 promised to send a lawagon and a Jr Marshall over to Townten to pick up the trail of Dianne Marmon's kidnapper as soon as the lawagon was free. Territory #22 promised the same, although they didn't think their car would be available until after nightfall. Clemens finally ordered his own Jr Marshall to fly over to Townten and do the best he could until a lawagon arrived. A live Jr Marshall sure as hell couldn't do much, though. Not what a lawagon could.

The little Townseven cafe he was calling from was fully automatic and Clemens sat down at a coffee table to wait for the repairman to arrive. The round light-blue room was empty except for a hunched old man who was sitting at a breakfast table, ordering side orders of hash browns one after another. When he'd filled the surface of the table he started a second layer. He didn't seem to be eating any of the food.

Clemens drank the cup of coffee that came up out of his table and ignored the old man. It was probably a case for a Psych Wagon but Clemens didn't feel up to going through the trouble of turning the man in. He finished his coffee. A car stopped outside and Clemens jumped. It was just a customer.

'How can I do that?' said the repairman as he and Clemens went down the ramp of the automatic cafe. 'Look.' He pointed across the parking area at his small one-man scooter.

Clemens shook his head. 'It's nearly sundown. A girl's life is in danger. Damn, if I have to wait here until you fix the lawagon and bring it back I'll lose that much more time.'

'I'm sorry,' said the small sun-worn man. 'I can't take you out to where the car is. The bureau says these scooters are not to carry passengers. So if I put more than 200 pounds on it it just turns off and won't go at all.'

'Okay, okay.' There were no cars in the parking lot, no one to commandeer.

'You told me where your lawagon is. I can find it if it's right on the highway. You wait.'

'How long?'

The repairman shrugged. 'Those babies don't break down much. But when they do. Could be a while. Overnight maybe.'

'Overnight?' Clemens grabbed the man's arm. 'You're kidding.'

'Don't break my damn arm or it'll take that much longer.'

'I'm sorry. I'll wait here. You'll drive the lawagon back?'

'Yeah. I got a special set of ID cards and passwords so I can get its hood up and drive it. Go inside and have a cup of coffee.'

'Sure,' said Clemens. 'Thanks.'

'Do my best.'

'Do you know anything about the dinner-for-two tables?' the thin loose-suited young man asked Clemens.

Clemens had taken the table nearest the door and was looking out at the twilight roadway. 'Beg pardon?'

'We put money in for a candle and nothing happened, except that when the asparagus arrived its ends were lit. This is my first date with this girl, marshall, and I want to make a good impression.'

'Hit the outlet with your fist,' said Clemens, turning away.

'Thank you, sir.'

Clemens got up and went in to call the Law Bureau answering service in Townten. The automatic voice told him that Jr Marshall Kepling had just arrived and reported in. He was on his way to the victim's apartment. No other news.

'She's not a victim,' said Clemens and cut off.

'Arrest those two,' said the old man, reaching for Clemens as he came out of the phone alcove.

'Why?'

'They shot a candle at my table and scattered my potatoes to here and gone.'

The young man ran up. 'I hit the table like you said and the candle came out. Only it went sailing all the way across the room.'

'Young people,' said the old man.

'Here,' said Clemens. He gave both of them some cash. 'Start all over again.'

'That's not,' started the old man.

Clemens saw something coming down the dark road. He pushed free and ran outside.

As he reached the roadway the lawagon slowed and stopped. There was no one inside.

'Welcome aboard,' said the car.

Clemens went through the identification ritual, looking off along the roadway, and got in. 'Where's the repairman? Did he send you on in alone?'

'I saw through him, sir,' said the lawagon. 'Shall we proceed to Townten?'

'Yes. Step on it,' said Clemens. 'But what do you mean you saw through him?'

The glove compartment dropped open. There were two white jars in it now. 'Sheldon Kloog won't bother us anymore, sir. I have just apprehended and tried him. He was disguised as a repairman and made an attempt to dismantle an official Law Bureau vehicle. That offence, plus his murder record, made only one course of action possible.'

Clemens swallowed, making himself not even tighten his grip on the wheel. If he said anything the car might stop again. There was something wrong. As soon as Dianne was safe Lawagon A10 would have to go into the shop for a thorough check-up. Right now Clemens needed the car badly, needed what it could do. They had to track down whoever had kidnapped Dianne. 'Good work,' he said evenly.

The headlights hit the cliffs that bordered the narrow road and long ragged shadows crept up the hillside ahead of them.

'I think we're closing in,' said Clemens. He was talking to Jr Marshall Kepling who he'd left back at the Law Bureau answering service in Townten. He had cautioned Kepling to make no mention of the Kloog business while the car could hear them.

'Central verified the ID on the kidnapper from the prints we found,' said Kepling. Surprisingly Kepling had found fingerprints in Dianne's apartment that the andy patrol and the mechanical deputy had missed. 'It is Jim Otterson. Up to now he's only done short sentence stuff.'

'Good,' said Clemens. That meant that Otterson might not harm Dianne. Unless this was the time he'd picked to cross over. 'The lawagon,' said Clemens, 'is holding onto his trail. We should get him now anytime. He's on foot now and the girl is definitely still with him the car says. We're closing in.'

'Good luck,' said Kepling.

'Thanks,' Clemens signed off.

Things had speeded up once he and the lawagon had reached Townten. Clemens had known that. The lawagon had had no trouble picking up the scent. Now, late at night, they were some twenty-five miles out of Townten. They'd found Otterson's car seven miles back with its clutch burned out. The auto had been there, off the unpaved back road, for about four hours. Otterson had driven around in great zigzags. Apparently he had spent the whole of the night after the kidnapping in a deserted storehouse about fifty miles from Townten. He had left there, according to the lawagon, about noon and headed towards Towneleven. Then he had doubled back again, swinging in near Townten. Clemens and the lawagon had spent hours circling around on Otterson's trail. With no more car Otterson and the girl couldn't have come much further than where Clemens and the lawagon were now.

The lawagon turned off the road and bumped across a rocky plateau. It swung around and stopped. Up above was a high flat cliff side, dotted with caves. 'Up there, I'd say,' said the lawagon. It had silenced its engine.

'Okay,' said Clemens. There wasn't much chance of sneaking up on Otterson if he was up in one of those caves. Clemens would have to risk trying to talk to him.

'Shoot the lights up there and turn on the speakers.'

Two spotlights hit the cliff and a hand mike came up out of the dash. Taking it, Clemens climbed out of the lawagon. 'Otterson, this is Marshall Clemens. I'm asking you to surrender. If you don't I'll have to use stun gas on you. We know you're in one of those caves and we can check each one off if we have to. Give up.'

Clemens waited. Then halfway up the cliff side something green flashed and then came hurtling down. It pinwheeled down the mountain and fell past the plateau.

'What the hell.' Clemens ran forward. There was a gully between the cliff and the plateau, narrow and about thirty feet deep. At its bottom now was something. It might be Dianne, arms tangled over interlaced brush.

'Get me a handlight and a line,' he called to the lawagon.

Without moving the car lobbed a handbeam to him and sent a thin cord snaking over the ground. 'Check.'

'Cover the caves. I'm going down to see what that was that fell.'

'Ready?'

Clemens hooked the light on his belt and gripped the line. He backed over the plateau edge. 'Okay, ready.'

The line was slowly let out and Clemens started down. Near the brush he caught a rock and let go of the line. He unhitched the light and swung it. He exhaled sharply. What had fallen was only an empty coat. Otterson was trying to decoy them. 'Watch out,' Clemens shouted to his car. 'It's not the girl. He may try to make a break now.'

He steadied himself and reached for the rope. Its end snapped out at him and before he could catch it it whirred up and out of sight. 'Hey, the rope. Send it back.'

'Emergency,' announced the lawagon, its engine coming on.

Up above a blaster sizzled and rock clattered. Clemens yanked out his pistol and looked up. Down the hillside a man was coming, carrying a bound-up girl in his arms.

His big hands showed and they held pistols. Dianne was gagged but seemed to be alive. Otterson zigzagged down, using the girl for a shield. He was firing not at Clemens but at the lawagon. He jumped across the gully to a plateau about twenty yards from where Clemens had started over.

Holstering his gun Clemens started to climb. He was half way up when he heard Otterson cry out. Then there was no sound at all.

Clemens tried to climb faster but could not. The gully side was jagged and hard to hold on to. Finally he swung himself up on the plateau.

'This is a public service announcement,' said the lawagon. 'Sheldon Kloog and his female accomplice have been captured, tried, sentenced, and executed. This message comes to you from the Law Bureau. Thank you.'

Clemens roared. He grabbed up a rock in each hand and went charging at the car. 'You've killed Dianne,' he shouted. 'You crazy damn machine.'

The lawagon turned and started rolling towards him. 'No you don't, Kloog,' it said.

The Case of the
Four and Twenty Blackbirds

Neil Gaiman

Neil Gaiman is one of those annoying people who does lots of things brilliantly. He made his name with his *Sandman* series of comic books. In 1990 he co-wrote *Good Omens* with Terry Pratchett, author of the *Discworld* series. He followed this up with the TV series *Neverwhere* (and the novel of the series). One of his latest books is *Smoke and Mirrors*.

In this story, he mixes up the hard-boiled detective story with a clutch of nursery rhymes, and gets characteristically crazy results.

I sat in my office, nursing a glass of **hooch** and idly cleaning my automatic. Outside the rain fell steadily, like it seems to do most of the time in our fair city, whatever the tourist board say. Hell, I didn't care. I'm not on the tourist board. I'm a private dick, and one of the best, although you wouldn't have known it; the office was crumbling, the rent was unpaid and the hooch was my last.

Things are tough all over.

To cap it all the only client I'd had all week never showed up on the street corner where I'd waited for him. He said it was going to be a big job, but now I'd never know: he kept a prior appointment in the morgue.

So when the dame walked into my office I was sure my luck had changed for the better.

'What are you selling, lady?'

---

hooch: an alcoholic drink, often whisky

She gave me a look that would have induced heavy breathing in a pumpkin, and which shot my heartbeat up to three figures. She had long blonde hair and a figure that would have made **Thomas Aquinas** forget his vows. I forgot all mine about never taking cases from dames.

'What would you say to some of the green stuff?' she asked in a husky voice, getting straight to the point.

'Continue, sister.' I didn't want her to know how bad I needed the dough, so I held my hand in front of my mouth; it doesn't help if a client sees you salivate.

She opened her purse and flipped out a photograph – a glossy eight by ten. 'Do you recognise that man?'

In my business you know who people are. 'Yeah.'

'He's dead.'

'I know that too, sweetheart. It's old news. It was an accident.'

Her gaze went so icy you could have chipped it into cubes and cooled a cocktail with it. 'My brother's death was no accident.'

I raised an eyebrow – you need a lot of **arcane** skills in my business – and said: 'Your brother, eh?' Funny, she hadn't struck me as the type that had brothers.

'I'm Jill Dumpty.'

'So your brother was Humpty Dumpty?'

'And he didn't fall off that wall, Mr Horner. He was pushed.'

Interesting, if true. Dumpty had his finger in most of the crooked pies in town; I could think of five guys who would have preferred to see him dead than alive without trying.

Without trying too hard, anyway.

'You seen the cops about this?'

Thomas Aquinas: a monk
arcane: secret, mysterious

'Nah. The King's Men aren't interested in anything to do with his death. They say they did all they could do in trying to put him together again after the fall.'

I leaned back in my chair.

'So what's it to you? Why do you need me?'

'I want you to find the killer, Mr Horner. I want him brought to justice. I want him to fry like an egg. Oh – and one other *little* thing,' she added, lightly. 'Before he died Humpty had a small **manila** envelope full of photographs he was meant to be sending me. Medical photos. I'm a trainee nurse, and I need them to pass my finals.'

I inspected my nails, then looked up at her face, taking in a handful of waist and Easter-egg bazonkas on the way up. She was a looker, although her cute nose was a little on the shiny side. 'I'll take the case. Seventy-five a day and two hundred bonus for results.'

She smiled; my stomach twisted around once and went into orbit. 'You get another two hundred if you get me those photographs. I want to be a nurse *real* bad.' Then she dropped three fifties on my desktop.

I let a devil-may-care grin play across my rugged face. 'Say, sister, how about letting me take you out for dinner? I just came into some money.'

She gave an involuntary shiver of anticipation and muttered something about having a thing about midgets, so I knew I was onto a good thing. Then she gave me a lopsided smile that would have made Albert Einstein drop a decimal point. 'First find my brother's killer, Mr Horner. And my photographs. *Then* we can play.'

She closed the door behind her. Maybe it was still raining but I didn't notice. I didn't care.

---

manila: strong (brown) paper

There are parts of town the tourist board don't mention. Parts of town where the police travel in threes if they travel at all. In my line of work you get to visit them more than is healthy. Healthy is never.

He was waiting for me outside Luigi's. I slid up behind him, my rubber-soled shoes soundless on the shiny wet sidewalk.

'Hiya, Cock.'

He jumped and spun round; I found myself gazing up into the muzzle of a .45. 'Oh, Horner.' He put the gun away. 'Don't call me Cock. I'm Bernie Robin to you, Short-stuff, and don't you forget it.'

'Cock Robin is good enough for me, Cock. Who killed Humpty Dumpty?'

He was a strange-looking bird, but you can't be choosy in my profession. He was the best underworld lead I had.

'Let's see the colour of your money.'

I showed him a fifty.

'Hell,' he muttered. 'It's green. Why can't they make puce or mauve money for a change?' He took it, though. 'All I know is that the Fat Man had his finger in a lot of pies.'

'So?'

'One of those pies had four and twenty blackbirds in it.'

'Huh?'

'Do I hafta spell it out for you? I . . . *Ughh* . . .' He crumpled to the sidewalk, an arrow protruding from his back. Cock Robin wasn't going to be doing any more chirping.

Sergeant O'Grady looked down at the body, then he looked down at me. 'Faith and begorrah, to be sure,' he said. 'If it isn't Little Jack Horner himself.'

'I didn't kill Cock Robin, Sarge.'

'And I suppose that the call we got down at the station telling us you were going to be rubbing the late Mr Robin out – here; tonight – was just a hoax?'

'If I'm the killer, where are my arrows?' I thumbed open a pack of gum and started to chew. 'It's a frame.'

He puffed on his **meerschaum** and then put it away, and idly played a couple of phrases of the *William Tell Overture* on his oboe. 'Maybe. Maybe not. But you're still a suspect. Don't leave town. And Horner . . .'

'Yeah?'

'Dumpty's death was an accident. That's what the coroner said. That's what I say. Drop the case.'

I thought about it. Then I thought of the money, and the girl. 'No dice, Sarge.'

He shrugged. 'It's your funeral.' He said it like it probably would be.

I had a funny feeling like he could be right.

'You're out of your depth, Horner. You're playing with the big boys. And it ain't healthy.'

From what I could remember of my schooldays he was correct. Whenever I played with the big boys I always wound up having the stuffing beaten out of me. But how did O'Grady – how *could* O'Grady have known that? Then I remembered something else.

O'Grady was the one that used to beat me up the most.

It was time for what we in the profession call 'legwork'. I made a few discreet enquiries around town, but found out nothing about Dumpty that I didn't know already.

Humpty Dumpty was a bad egg. I remembered him when he was new in town, a smart young animal trainer with a nice line in training mice to run up clocks. He went to the bad pretty fast though; gambling, drink, women, it's the same story all over. A bright young kid thinks that the streets of Nurseryland are paved with gold, and by the time he finds out otherwise it's much too late.

---

meerschaum: a white clay; here, a pipe made from it

Dumpty started off with extortions and robbery on a small scale – he trained up a team of spiders to scare little girls away from their curds and whey, which he'd pick up and sell on the black market. Then he moved on to blackmail – the nastiest game. We crossed paths once, when I was hired by this young society kid – let's call him Georgie Porgie – to recover some compromising snaps of him kissing the girls and making them cry. I got the snaps, but I learned it wasn't healthy to mess with the Fat Man. And I don't make the same mistakes twice. Hell, in my line of work I can't afford to make the same mistakes once.

It's a tough world out there. I remember when Little Bo Peep first came to town . . . but you don't want to hear my troubles. If you're not dead yet, you've got troubles of your own.

I checked out the newspaper files on Dumpty's death. One minute he was sitting on a wall, the next he was in pieces at the bottom. All the King's Horses and all the King's Men were on the scene in minutes, but he needed more than first aid. A medic named Foster was called – a friend of Dumpty's from his Gloucester days – although I don't know of anything a doc can do when you're dead.

Hang on a second – *Dr Foster!*

I got that old feeling you get in my line of work. Two little brain cells rub together the right way and in seconds you've got a 24-carat **cerebral** fire on your hands.

You remember the client who didn't show – the one I'd waited for all day on the street corner? An accidental death. I hadn't bothered to check it out – I can't afford to waste time on clients who aren't going to pay for it.

Three deaths, it seemed. Not one.

I reached for the telephone and rang the police station.

---

cerebral: to do with the brain

'This is Horner,' I told the desk man. 'Lemme speak to Sergeant O'Grady.'

There was a crackling and he came on the line. 'O'Grady speaking.'

'It's Horner.'

'Hi, Little Jack.' That was just like O'Grady. He'd been kidding me about my size since we were kids together. 'You finally figured out that Dumpty's death was an accident?'

'Nope. I'm now investigating three deaths. The Fat Man's, Bernie Robin's and Dr Foster's.'

'Foster the plastic surgeon? His death was an accident.'

'Sure. And your mother was married to your father.'

There was a pause. 'Horner, if you phoned me up just to talk dirty, I'm not amused.'

'Okay, wise guy. If Humpty Dumpty's death was an accident and so was Dr Foster's, tell me just one thing.

'Who killed Cock Robin?'

I don't ever get accused of having too much imagination, but there's one thing I'd swear to. I could *hear* him grinning over the phone as he said: 'You did, Horner. And I'm staking my badge on it.'

The line went dead.

My office was cold and lonely, so I wandered down to Joe's Bar for some companionship and a drink or three.

Four and twenty blackbirds. A dead doctor. The Fat Man. Cock Robin . . . Heck, this case had more holes in it than a Swiss cheese and more loose ends than a torn string vest. And where did the juicy Miss Dumpty come into it? Jack and Jill – we'd make a great team. When this was all over perhaps we could go off together to Louie's little place on the hill, where no one's interested in whether you got a marriage licence or not. 'The Pail of Water', that was the name of the joint.

I called over the bartender. 'Hey. Joe.'

'Yeah, Mr Horner?' He was polishing a glass with a rag that had seen better days as a shirt.

'Did you ever meet the Fat Man's sister?'

He scratched at his cheek. 'Can't say as I did. His sister . . . huh? Hey – the Fat Man didn't have a sister.'

'You sure of that?'

'Sure I'm sure. It was the day my sister had her first kid – I told the Fat Man I was an uncle. He gave me this look and says, "Ain't no way I'll ever be an uncle, Joe. Got no sisters or brothers, nor no other kinfolk neither".'

If the mysterious Miss Dumpty wasn't his sister, who *was* she?

'Tell me, Joe. Didja ever see him in here with a dame – about so high, shaped like this?' My hands described a couple of **parabolas**. 'Looks like a blonde love goddess.'

He shook his head. 'Never saw him with any dames. Recently he was hanging around with some medical guy, but the only thing he ever cared about was those crazy birds and animals of his.'

I took a swig of my drink. It nearly took the roof of my mouth off. 'Animals? I thought he'd given all that up.'

'Naw – couple weeks back he was in here with a whole bunch of blackbirds he was training to sing "Wasn't that a dainty dish to set before *Mmm Mmm*".'

'*Mmm Mmm*?'

'Yeah. I got no idea who.'

I put my drink down. A little of it spilt on the counter, and I watched it strip the varnish. 'Thanks, Joe. You've been a big help.' I handed him a ten-dollar bill. 'For information received,' I said, adding, 'Don't spend it all at once.'

In my profession it's making little jokes like that that keeps you sane.

---

parabola: a curve

I had one contact left. I found a pay phone and called her number.

'Old Mother Hubbard's Cupboard – Cake Shop and Licensed Soup Kitchen.'

'It's Horner, Ma.'

'Jack? It ain't safe for me to talk to you.'

'For old time's sake, sweetheart. You owe me a favour.' Some two-bit crooks had once knocked off the Cupboard, leaving it bare. I'd tracked them down and returned the cakes and soup.

' . . . Okay. But I don't like it.'

'*You* know everything that goes on around here on the food front, Ma. What's the significance of a pie with four and twenty trained blackbirds in it?'

She whistled, long and low. 'You really don't know?'

'I wouldn't be asking you if I did.'

'You should read the Court pages of the papers next time, sugar. Jeez. You are out of your depth.'

'C'mon, Ma. Spill it.'

'It so happens that that particular dish was set before the King a few weeks back . . . Jack? Are you still there?'

'I'm still here, ma'am,' I said, quietly. 'All of a sudden a lot of things are starting to make sense.' I put down the phone.

It was beginning to look like Little Jack Horner had pulled out a plum from this pie.

It was raining, steady and cold.

I phoned a cab.

Quarter of an hour later one lurched out of the darkness.

'You're late.'

'So complain to the tourist board.'

I climbed in the back, wound down the window, and lit a cigarette.

And I went to see the Queen.

The door to the private part of the palace was locked. It's the part that the public don't get to see. But I've never been public, and the little lock hardly slowed me up. The door to the private apartments with the big red heart on it was unlocked, so I knocked and walked straight in.

The Queen of Hearts was alone, standing in front of the mirror, holding a plate of jam tarts with one hand, powdering her nose with the other. She turned, saw me, and gasped, dropping the tarts.

'Hey, Queenie,' I said. 'Or would you feel more comfortable if I called you Jill?'

She was still a good-looking slice of dame, even without the blonde wig.

'Get out of here!' she hissed.

'I don't think so, toots.' I sat down on the bed. 'Let me spell a few things out for you.'

'Go ahead.' She reached behind her for a concealed alarm button. I let her press it. I'd cut the wires on my way in – in my profession there's no such thing as being too careful.

'Let me spell a few things out for you.'

'You just said that.'

'I'll tell this my way, lady.'

I lit a cigarette and a thin plume of blue smoke drifted heavenwards, which was where I was going if my hunch was wrong. Still, I've learned to trust hunches.

'Try this on for size. Dumpty – the Fat Man – wasn't your brother. He wasn't even your friend. In fact he was blackmailing you. He knew about your nose.'

She turned whiter than a number of corpses I've met in my time in the business. Her hand reached up and cradled her freshly powdered nose.

'You see, I've known the Fat Man for many years, and many years ago he had a lucrative concern in training animals and birds to do certain unsavoury things. And that got me to thinking . . . I had a client recently who didn't show, due to his having been stiffed first. Doctor Foster, of Gloucester, the plastic surgeon. The official version of his death was that he'd just sat too close to a fire and melted.

'But just suppose he was killed to stop him telling something that he knew? I put two and two together and hit the jackpot. Let me reconstruct a scene for you: You were out in the garden – probably hanging out some clothes – when along came one of Dumpty's trained pie-blackbirds and *pecked off your nose*.

'So there you were, standing in the garden, your hand in front of your face, when along comes the Fat Man with an offer you couldn't refuse. He could introduce you to a plastic surgeon who could fix you up with a nose as good as new, for a price. And no one need ever know. Am I right so far?'

She nodded dumbly, then finding her voice, muttered: 'Pretty much. But I ran back into the parlour after the attack, to eat some bread and honey. That was where he found me.'

'Fair enough.' The colour was starting to come back into her cheeks now. 'So you had the operation from Foster, and no one was going to be any the wiser. Until Dumpty told you that he had photos of the op. You had to get rid of him. A couple of days later you were out walking in the palace grounds. There was Humpty, sitting on a wall, his back to you, gazing out into the distance. In a fit of madness, you pushed. And Humpty Dumpty had a great fall.

'But now you were in big trouble. Nobody suspected you of his murder, but where were the photographs? Foster didn't have them, although he smelled a rat and had to be disposed of – before he could see me. But you didn't know how much he'd told me, and you still didn't have the snapshots, so you took me on to find out. And that was your mistake, sister.'

Her lower lip trembled, and my heart quivered. 'You won't turn me in, will you?'

'Sister, you tried to frame me this afternoon. I don't take kindly to that.'

With a shaking hand she started to unbutton her blouse. 'Perhaps we could come to some sort of arrangement?'

I shook my head. 'Sorry, Your Majesty. Mrs Horner's little boy Jack was always taught to keep his hands off royalty. It's a pity, but that's how it is.' To be on the safe side I looked away, which was a mistake. A cute little ladies' pistol was in her hands and pointing at me before you could sing a song of sixpence. The shooter may have been small, but I knew it packed enough of a wallop to take me out of the game permanently.

This dame was *lethal*.

'Put that gun down, Your Majesty.' Sergeant O'Grady strolled through the bedroom door, his police special clutched in his ham-like fist.

'I'm sorry I suspected you, Horner,' he said dryly. 'You're lucky I did, though, sure and begorrah. I had you trailed here and I overheard the whole thing.'

'Hi, Sarge, thanks for stopping by. But I hadn't finished my explanation. If you'll take a seat I'll wrap it up.'

He nodded brusquely, and sat down near the door. His gun hardly moved.

I got up from the bed and walked over to the Queen. 'You see, toots, what I didn't tell you was who *did* have the snaps of your nose job. Humpty did, when you killed him.'

A charming frown crinkled her perfect brow. 'I don't understand . . . I had the body searched.'

'Sure, afterwards. But the first people to get to the Fat Man were the King's Men. The cops. And one of them pocketed the envelope. When any fuss had died down the blackmail would have started again. Only this time you wouldn't have known who to kill. And I owe you an apology.' I bent down to tie my shoelaces.

'Why?'

'I accused you of trying to frame me this afternoon. You didn't. That arrow was the property of a boy who was the best archer in my school – I should have recognised that distinctive **fletching** anywhere. Isn't that right,' I said, turning back to the door, ' . . . "Sparrow" O'Grady?'

Under the guise of tying up my shoelaces I had already palmed a couple of the Queen's jam tarts, and, flinging one of them upwards, I neatly smashed the room's only light bulb.

It only delayed the shooting a few seconds, but a few seconds was all I needed, and as the Queen of Hearts and Sergeant 'Sparrow' O'Grady cheerfully shot each other to bits, I split.

In my business, you have to look after number one.

Munching on a jam tart I walked out of the palace grounds and into the street. I paused by a trash-can, to try to burn the manila envelope of photographs I had pulled from O'Grady's pocket as I walked past him, but it was raining so hard they wouldn't catch.

When I got back to my office I phoned the tourist board to complain. They said the rain was good for the farmers, and I told them what they could do with it.

They said that things are tough all over.

And I said. Yeah.

---

fletching: pattern of feathers on an arrow

The Fifty-first Dragon
Heywood Broun

Heywood Broun was an American humourist who wrote for many newspapers. He was never a mainstream science-fiction and fantasy author, and his work is hard to come by. This is a pity, because in this story he shows just how funny he could be. What can you do with a 'knight in armour' who happens to be a chicken? Can magic make a knight brave and bold? Or is it all in the mind?

Of all the pupils at the knight school Gawaine le Cœur-Hardy was among the least promising. He was tall and sturdy, but his instructors soon discovered that he lacked spirit. He would hide in the woods when the jousting class was called, although his companions and members of the faculty sought to appeal to his better nature by shouting to him to come out and break his neck like a man. Even when they told him that the lances were padded, the horses no more than ponies and the field unusually soft for late autumn, Gawaine refused to grow enthusiastic. The Headmaster and the Assistant Professor of Pleasaunce were discussing the case one spring afternoon and the Assistant Professor could see no remedy but expulsion.

'No,' said the Headmaster, as he looked out at the purple hills which ringed the school, 'I think I'll train him to slay dragons.'

'He might be killed,' objected the Assistant Professor.

'So he might,' replied the Headmaster brightly, but he added, more soberly, 'we must consider the greater good. We are responsible for the formation of this lad's character.'

'Are the dragons particularly bad this year?' interrupted the Assistant Professor. This was characteristic. He always seemed restive when the head of the school began to talk ethics and the ideals of the institution.

'I've never known them worse,' replied the Headmaster. 'Up in the hills to the south last week they killed a number of peasants, two cows and a prize pig. And if this dry spell holds there's no telling when they may start a forest fire simply by breathing around indiscriminately.'

'Would any refund on the tuition fee be necessary in case of an accident to young Cœur-Hardy?'

'No,' the principal answered, judicially, 'that's all covered in the contract. But as a matter of fact he won't be killed. Before I send him up in the hills I'm going to give him a magic word.'

'That's a good idea,' said the Professor. 'Sometimes they work wonders.'

From that day on Gawaine specialised in dragons. His course included both theory and practice. In the morning there were long lectures on the history, anatomy, manners and customs of dragons. Gawaine did not distinguish himself in these studies. He had a marvellously versatile gift for forgetting things. In the afternoon he showed to better advantage, for then he would go down to the South Meadow and practise with a battleaxe. In this exercise he was truly impressive, for he had enormous strength as well as speed and grace. He even developed a deceptive display of ferocity. Old alumni say that it was a thrilling sight to see Gawaine charging across the field towards the dummy paper dragon which had been set up for his practice. As he ran he would brandish his axe and shout 'A murrain on thee!' or some other vivid bit of campus slang. It never took him more than one stroke to behead the dummy dragon.

Gradually his task was made more difficult. Paper gave way to papier-mâché and finally to wood, but even the toughest of these dummy dragons had no terrors for Gawaine. One sweep of the axe always did the business. There were those who said that when the practice was protracted until dusk and the dragons threw long, fantastic shadows across the meadow Gawaine did not charge so impetuously nor shout so loudly. It is possible there was malice in this charge. At any rate, the Headmaster decided by the end of June that it was time for the test. Only the night before a dragon had come close to the school grounds and had eaten some of the lettuce from the garden. The faculty decided that Gawaine was ready. They gave him a diploma and a new battleaxe and the Headmaster summoned him to a private conference.

'Sit down,' said the Headmaster. 'Have a cigarette.'

Gawaine hesitated.

'Oh, I know it's against the rules,' said the Headmaster. 'But after all, you have received your preliminary degree. You are no longer a boy. You are a man. Tomorrow you will go out into the world, the great world of achievement.'

Gawaine took a cigarette. The Headmaster offered him a match, but he produced one of his own and began to puff away with a dexterity which quite amazed the principal.

'Here you have learned the theories of life,' continued the Headmaster, resuming the thread of his discourse, 'but after all, life is not a matter of theories. Life is a matter of facts. It calls on the young and the old alike to face these facts, even though they are hard and sometimes unpleasant. Your problem, for example, is to slay dragons.'

'They say that those dragons down in the south wood are 500 feet long,' ventured Gawaine, timorously.

'Stuff and nonsense!' said the Headmaster. 'The curate saw one last week from the top of Arthur's Hill. The dragon was sunning himself down in the valley.

The curate didn't have an opportunity to look at him very long because he felt it was his duty to hurry back to make a report to me. He said the monster, or shall I say, the big lizard? – wasn't an inch over 200 feet. But the size has nothing at all to do with it. You'll find the big ones even easier than the little ones. They're far slower on their feet and less aggressive, I'm told. Besides, before you go I'm going to equip you in such fashion that you need have no fear of all the dragons in the world.'

'I'd like an enchanted cap,' said Gawaine.

'What's that?' answered the Headmaster, testily.

'A cap to make me disappear,' explained Gawaine.

The Headmaster laughed indulgently. 'You mustn't believe all those old wives' stories,' he said. 'There isn't any such thing. A cap to make you disappear, indeed! What would you do with it? You haven't even appeared yet. Why, my boy, you could walk from here to London, and nobody would so much as look at you. You're nobody. You couldn't be more invisible than that.'

Gawaine seemed dangerously close to a relapse into his old habit of whimpering. The Headmaster reassured him: 'Don't worry; I'll give you something much better than an enchanted cap. I'm going to give you a magic word. All you have to do is to repeat this magic charm once and no dragon can possibly harm a hair of your head. You can cut off his head at your leisure.'

He took a heavy book from the shelf behind his desk and began to run through it. 'Sometimes,' he said, 'the charm is a whole phrase or even a sentence. I might, for instance, give you "To make the" – No, that might not do. I think a single word would be best for dragons.'

'A short word,' suggested Gawaine.

'It can't be too short or it wouldn't be potent. There isn't so much hurry as all that. Here's a splendid magic word: "Rumplesnitz". Do you think you can learn that?'

Gawaine tried and in an hour or so he seemed to have the word well in hand. Again and again he interrupted the lesson to inquire, 'And if I say "Rumplesnitz" the dragon can't possibly hurt me?' And always the Headmaster replied, 'If you only say "Rumplesnitz", you are perfectly safe.'

Towards morning Gawaine seemed resigned to his career. At daybreak the Headmaster saw him to the edge of the forest and pointed him to the direction in which he should proceed. About a mile away to the south-west a cloud of steam hovered over an open meadow in the woods and the Headmaster assured Gawaine that under the steam he would find a dragon. Gawaine went forward slowly. He wondered whether it would be best to approach the dragon on the run as he did in his practice in the South Meadow or to walk slowly towards him, shouting 'Rumplesnitz' all the way.

The problem was decided for him. No sooner had he come to the fringe of the meadow than the dragon spied him and began to charge. It was a large dragon and yet it seemed decidedly aggressive in spite of the Headmaster's statement to the contrary. As the dragon charged it released huge clouds of hissing steam through its nostrils. It was almost as if a gigantic teapot had gone mad.

The dragon came forward so fast and Gawaine was so frightened that he had time to say 'Rumplesnitz' only once. As he said it, he swung his battleaxe and off popped the head of the dragon. Gawaine had to admit that it was even easier to kill a real dragon than a wooden one if only you said 'Rumplesnitz'.

Gawaine brought the ears home and a small section of the tail. His schoolmates and the faculty made much of him, but the Headmaster wisely kept him from being spoiled by insisting that he go on with his work. Every clear day Gawaine rose at dawn and went out to kill dragons. The Headmaster kept him at home when it rained, because he said the woods were damp and unhealthy at such times and that he didn't want the boy to run needless risks. Few good days passed in which Gawaine failed to get a dragon. On one particularly fortunate day he killed three, a husband and wife and a visiting relative. Gradually he developed a technique. Pupils who sometimes watched him from the hilltops a long way off said that he often allowed the dragon to come within a few feet before he said 'Rumplesnitz'. He came to say it with a mocking sneer. Occasionally he did stunts. Once when an excursion party from London was watching him he went into action with his right hand tied behind his back. The dragon's head came off just as easily.

As Gawaine's record of killings mounted higher the Headmaster found it impossible to keep him completely in hand. He fell into the habit of stealing out at night and engaging in long drinking bouts at the village tavern. It was after such a **debauch** that he rose a little before dawn one fine August morning and started out after his fiftieth dragon. His head was heavy and his mind sluggish. He was heavy in other respects as well, for he had adopted the somewhat vulgar practice of wearing his medals, ribbons and all, when he went out dragon hunting. The decorations began on his chest and ran all the way down to his abdomen. They must have weighed at least eight pounds.

Gawaine found a dragon in the same meadow where he had killed the first one. It was a fair-sized dragon, but evidently an old one. Its face was wrinkled and Gawaine thought he had never seen so hideous a countenance. Much to the lad's disgust, the monster refused to charge and Gawaine was obliged to walk towards him. He whistled as he went. The dragon regarded him hopelessly, but craftily. Of course it had heard of Gawaine. Even when the lad raised his battleaxe the dragon made no move. It knew that there was no salvation in the quickest thrust of the head, for it had been informed that this hunter was protected by an enchantment. It merely waited, hoping something would turn up. Gawaine raised the battleaxe and suddenly lowered it again. He had grown very pale and he trembled violently. The dragon suspected a trick. 'What's the matter?' it asked, with false solicitude.

'I've forgotten the magic word,' stammered Gawaine.

'What a pity,' said the dragon. 'So that was the secret. It doesn't seem quite sporting to me, all this magic stuff, you know. Not cricket, as we used to say when I was a little dragon; but after all, that's a matter of opinion.'

Gawaine was so helpless with terror that the dragon's confidence rose immeasurably and it could not resist the temptation to show off a bit.

---

debauch: a drunken party or orgy

'Could I possibly be of any assistance?' it asked. 'What's the first letter of the magic word?'

'It begins with an "r",' said Gawaine weakly.

'Let's see,' mused the dragon, 'that doesn't tell us much, does it? What sort of a word is this? Is it an **epithet**, do you think?'

Gawaine could do no more than nod.

'Why, of course,' exclaimed the dragon, 'reactionary Republican.'

Gawaine shook his head.

'Well, then,' said the dragon, 'we'd better get down to business. Will you surrender?'

With the suggestion of a compromise Gawaine mustered up enough courage to speak.

'What will you do if I surrender?' he asked.

'Why, I'll eat you,' said the dragon.

'And if I don't surrender?'

'I'll eat you just the same.'

'Then it doesn't make any difference, does it?' moaned Gawaine.

'It does to me,' said the dragon with a smile. 'I'd rather you didn't surrender. You'd taste much better if you didn't.'

The dragon waited for a long time for Gawaine to ask 'Why?' but the boy was too frightened to speak. At last the dragon had to give the explanation without his cue line. 'You see,' he said, 'if you don't surrender you'll taste better because you'll die game.'

This was an old and ancient trick of the dragon's. By means of some such quip he was accustomed to paralyse his victims with laughter and then to destroy them. Gawaine was sufficiently paralysed as it was, but laughter had no part in his helplessness. With the last word of the joke the dragon drew back his head and struck. In that

---

epithet: a descriptive term; an adjective describing a quality

second there flashed into the mind of Gawaine the magic word 'Rumplesnitz', but there was no time to say it. There was time only to strike and, without a word, Gawaine met the onrush of the dragon with a full swing. He put all his back and shoulders into it. The impact was terrific and the head of the dragon flew away almost a hundred yards and landed in a thicket.

Gawaine did not remain frightened very long after the death of the dragon. His mood was one of wonder. He was enormously puzzled. He cut off the ears of the monster almost in a trance. Again and again he thought to himself, 'I didn't say "Rumplesnitz"!' He was sure of that and yet, there was no question that he had killed the dragon. In fact, he had never killed one so utterly. Never before had he driven a head for anything like the same distance. Twenty-five yards was perhaps his best previous record. All the way back to the knight school he kept rumbling about in his mind seeking an explanation for what had occurred. He went to the Headmaster immediately and after closing the door told him what had happened. 'I didn't say "Rumpelsnitz",' he explained with great earnestness.

The Headmaster laughed. 'I'm glad you've found out,' he said. 'It makes you ever so much more of a hero. Don't you see that? Now you know that it was you who killed all these dragons and not that foolish little word "Rumplesnitz".'

Gawaine frowned. 'Then it wasn't a magic word after all?' he asked.

'Of course not,' said the Headmaster, 'you ought to be too old for such foolishness. There isn't any such thing as a magic word.'

'But you told me it was magic,' protested Gawaine. 'You said it was magic and now you say it isn't.'

'It wasn't magic in a literal sense,' answered the Headmaster, 'but it was much more wonderful than that. The word gave you confidence. It took away your fears. If

I hadn't told you that you might have been killed the very first time. It was your battleaxe did the trick.'

Gawaine surprised the Headmaster by his attitude. He was obviously distressed by the explanation. He interrupted a long philosophic and ethical discourse by the Headmaster with, 'If I hadn't of hit 'em all mighty hard and fast any one of 'em might have crushed me like a, like a –' He fumbled for a word.

'Egg shell,' suggested the Headmaster.

'Like a egg shell,' assented Gawaine, and he said it many times. All through the evening meal people who sat near him heard him muttering, 'Like a egg shell, like a egg shell.'

The next day was clear, but Gawaine did not get up at dawn. Indeed, it was almost noon when the Headmaster found him cowering in bed, with the clothes pulled over his head. The principal called the Assistant Professor of Pleasaunce, and together they dragged the boy towards the forest.

'He'll be all right as soon as he gets a couple more dragons under his belt,' explained the Headmaster.

The Assistant Professor of Pleasaunce agreed. 'It would be a shame to stop such a fine run,' he said. 'Why, counting that one yesterday, he's killed 50 dragons.'

They pushed the boy into a thicket above which hung a meagre cloud of steam. It was obviously quite a small dragon. But Gawaine did not come back that night or the next. In fact, he never came back. Some weeks afterwards, brave spirits from the school explored the thicket, but they could find nothing to remind them of Gawaine except the metal part of his medals. Even the ribbons had been devoured.

The Headmaster and the Assistant Professor of Pleasaunce agreed that it would be just as well not to tell the school how Gawaine had achieved his record and still less how he came to die. They held that it might have a bad effect on school spirit. Accordingly, Gawaine has lived in the memory of the school as its greatest hero. No visitor succeeds in leaving the building today without seeing a great shield which hangs on the wall of the dining hall. Fifty pairs of dragons' ears are mounted upon the shield and underneath in gilt letters is 'Gawaine le Cœur-Hardy,' followed by the simple inscription, 'He killed 50 dragons.' The record has never been equalled.

Into Your Tent I'll Creep

Eric Frank Russell

Though he made his name in American sci-fi magazines such as *Astounding*, Eric Frank Russell is a British writer. He is also one of the funniest and most humane writers in the whole of science fiction.

His best-known books are *Sinister Barrier* and the hilarious *Next of Kin*, but his best work is in his short stories, and they are well worth searching out.

Are human beings really the most intelligent species on Earth? Douglas Adams, in *The Hitch Hiker's Guide to the Galaxy*, reckons that there are at least two more intelligent species than us – dolphins, and mice. Eric Frank Russell offers a different theory . . .

Morfad sat in the midship cabin and gloomed at the wall. He was worried and couldn't conceal the fact. The present situation had the frustrating qualities of a gigantic rat trap. One could escape it only with the combined help of all the other rats.

But the others weren't likely to lift a finger either on his or their own behalf. He felt sure of that. How can you persuade people to try to escape a jam when you can't convince them that they're in it, right up to the neck?

A rat runs around a trap only because he is grimly aware of its existence. So long as he remains blissfully ignorant of it, he does nothing. On this very world a horde of intelligent aliens had done nothing about it through the whole of their history. Fifty sceptical Altairans weren't likely to step in where three thousand million Terrans had failed.

He was still sitting there when Haraka came in and informed, 'We leave at sunset.'

Morfad said nothing.

'I'll be sorry to go,' added Haraka. He was the ship's captain, a big, burly sample of Altairan life. Rubbing flexible fingers together, he went on, 'We've been lucky to discover this planet, exceedingly lucky. We've become blood brothers of a life form fully up to our own standard of intelligence, space-traversing like ourselves, friendly and co-operative.'

Morfad said nothing.

'Their reception of us has been most cordial,' Haraka continued enthusiastically. 'Our people will be greatly heartened when they hear our report. A great future lies before us, no doubt of that. A Terran–Altairan combine will be invincible. Between us we can explore and exploit the entire galaxy.'

Morfad said nothing.

Cooling down, Haraka frowned at him. 'What's the matter with you, Misery?'

'I am not overjoyed.'

'I can see that much. Your face resembles a very sour *shamsid* on an aged and withered bush. And at a time of triumph, too! Are you ill?'

'No.' Turning slowly, Morfad looked him straight in the eyes. 'Do you believe in psionic faculties?'

Haraka reacted as if caught on one foot. 'Well, I don't know. I am a captain, a trained engineer-navigator, and as such I cannot pretend to be an expert upon extraordinary abilities. You ask me something I am not qualified to answer. How about you? Do you believe in them?'

'I do – *now*.'

'Now? Why now?'

'The belief has been thrust upon me.' Morfad hesitated, went on with a touch of desperation. 'I have discovered that I am telepathic.'

Surveying him with slight incredulity, Haraka said, 'You've discovered it? You mean it has come upon you recently?'

'Yes.'

'Since when?'

'Since we arrived on Terra.'

'I don't understand this at all,' confessed Haraka, baffled. 'Do you assert that some peculiarity in Terra's conditions has suddenly enabled you to read my thoughts?'

'No, I cannot read your thoughts.'

'But you've just said that you have become telepathic.'

'So I have. I can hear thoughts as clearly as if the words were being shouted aloud. But not your thoughts nor those of any member of our crew.'

Haraka leaned forward, his features intent. 'Ah, you have been hearing *Terran* thoughts, eh? And what you've heard has got you bothered? Morfad, I am your captain, your commander. It is your bounden duty to tell me of anything suspicious about these Terrans.' He waited a bit, urged impatiently, 'Come on, speak up!'

'I know no more about these humanoids than you do,' said Morfad. 'I have every reason to believe them genuinely friendly but I don't know what they think.'

'But by the stars, man, you –'

'We are talking at cross-purposes,' Morfad interrupted. 'Whether I do or do not overhear Terran thoughts depends upon what one means by Terrans.'

'Look,' said Haraka, 'whose thoughts *do* you hear?'

Steeling himself, Morfad said flatly, 'Those of Terran dogs.'

'Dogs?' Haraka lay back and stared at him. '*Dogs?* Are you serious?'

'I have never been more so. I can hear dogs and no others. Don't ask me why because I don't know. It is a freak of circumstance.'

'And you have listened to their minds ever since we jumped to Earth?'

'Yes.'

'What sort of things have you heard?'

'I have had pearls of alien wisdom cast before me,' declared Morfad, 'and the longer I look at them the more they scare hell out of me.'

'Get busy frightening me with a few examples,' invited Haraka, suppressing a smile.

'Quote: the supreme test of intelligence is the ability to live as one pleases without working,' recited Morfad. 'Quote: the art of retribution is that of concealing it beyond all suspicion. Quote: the sharpest, most subtle, most effective weapon in the cosmos is flattery.'

'Huh?'

'Quote: if a thing can think it likes to think that it is God – treat it as God and it becomes your willing slave.'

'Oh, no!' denied Haraka.

'Oh, *yes!*' insisted Morfad. He waved a hand towards the nearest port. 'Out there are three thousand million petty gods. They are eagerly panted after, fawned upon, gazed upon with worshipping eyes. Gods are very gracious towards those who love them.' He made a spitting sound that lent emphasis to what followed. 'The lovers know it – and love comes cheap.'

Haraka said, uneasily, 'I think you're crazy.'

'Quote: to rule successfully the ruled must be unconscious of it.' Again the spitting sound. 'Is that crazy? I don't think so. It makes sense. It works. It's working out there right now.'

'But –'

'Take a look at this.' He tossed a small object into Haraka's lap. 'Recognise it?'

'Yes, it's what they call a cracker.'

'Correct. To make it some Terrans ploughed fields in all kinds of weather, rain, wind and sunshine, sowed wheat, reaped it with the aid of machinery other Terrans had sweated to build. They transported the wheat, stored it, milled it, enriched the flour by various processes, baked it, packaged it, shipped it all over the world. When humanoid Terrans want crackers they've got to put in man-hours to get them.'

'So –'

'When a dog wants one he sits up, waves his forepaws and admires his god. That's all. Just that.'

'But, darn it, man, dogs are relatively stupid.'

'So it seems,' said Morfad, drily.

'They can't really *do* anything effective.'

'That depends upon what one regards as effective.'

'They haven't got hands.'

'And don't need them – having brains.'

'Now see here,' declaimed Haraka, openly irritated, 'we Altairans invented and constructed ships capable of roaming the spaces between the stars. The Terrans have done the same. Terran dogs have not done it and won't do it in the next million years. When one dog has the brains and ability to get to another planet I'll eat my cap.'

'You can do that right now,' Morfad suggested. 'We have two dogs on board.'

Haraka let go a grunt of disdain. 'The Terrans have given us those as a memento.'

'Sure they gave them to us – at whose **behest**?'

'It was wholly a spontaneous gesture.'

'Was it?'

'Are you suggesting that dogs put the idea into their heads?' Haraka demanded.

'I know they did,' retorted Morfad, looking grim. 'And we've not been given two males or two females. Oh no, sir, not on your life. One male and one female. The givers said we could breed them. Thus in due course our own

---

behest: a command

worlds can become illuminated with the undying love of man's best friend.'

'Nuts!' said Haraka.

Morfad gave back, 'You're obsessed with the old, out-of-date idea that conquest must be preceded by aggression. Can't you understand that a wholly alien species just naturally uses wholly alien methods? Dogs employ their own tactics, not ours. It isn't within their nature or abilities to take us over with the aid of ships, guns and a great hullabaloo. It *is* within their nature and abilities to creep in upon us, their eyes shining with hero-worship. If we don't watch out, we'll be mastered by a horde of loving creepers.'

'I can invent a word for your mental condition,' said Haraka. 'You're suffering from caniphobia.'

'With good reasons.'

'Imaginary ones.'

'Yesterday I looked into a dogs' beauty shop. Who was doing the bathing, scenting, powdering, primping? Other dogs? Hah! Humanoid females were busy dolling 'em up. Was *that* imaginary?'

'You can call it a Terran eccentricity. It means nothing whatever. Besides, we've quite a few funny habits of our own.'

'You're dead right there,' Morfad agreed. 'And I know one of yours. So does the entire crew.'

Haraka narrowed his eyes. 'You might as well name it. I am not afraid to see myself as others see me.'

'All right. You've asked for it. You think a lot of Kashim. He always has your ear. You will listen to him when you'll listen to nobody else. Everything he says makes sound sense – to you.'

'So you're jealous of Kashim, eh?'

'Not in the least,' assured Morfad, making a disparaging gesture. 'I merely despise him for the same reason that everyone else holds him in contempt. He is a professional toady. He spends most of his time fawning upon you, flattering you, pandering to your ego. He is a natural-born creeper who gives you the Terradog treatment. You like it. You bask in it. It affects you like an irresistible drug. It works – and don't tell me that it doesn't because all of us know that it *does*.'

'I am not a fool. I have Kashim sized up. He does not influence me to the extent you believe.'

'Three thousand million Terrans have four hundred million dogs sized up and are equally convinced that no dog has a say in anything worth a hoot.'

'I don't believe it.'

'Of course you don't. I had little hope that you would. Morfad is telling you these things and Morfad is either crazy or a liar. But if Kashim were to tell you while prostrate at the foot of your throne you would swallow his story hook, line and sinker. Kashim has a Terradog mind and uses Terradog logic, see?'

'My disbelief has better basis than that.'

'For instance?' Morfad invited.

'Some Terrans are telepathic. Therefore if this myth of subtle mastery by dogs were a fact, they'd know of it. Not a dog would be left alive on this world.' Haraka paused, finished pointedly, 'They don't know of it.'

'Terran telepaths hear the minds of their own kind but not those of dogs. I hear the minds of dogs but not those of any other kind. As I said before, I don't know why this should be. I know only that it *is*.'

'It seems nonsensical to me.'

'It would. I suppose you can't be blamed for taking that viewpoint. My position is difficult; I'm like the only one with ears in a world that is stone-deaf.'

Haraka thought it over, said after a while, 'Suppose I were to accept everything you've said at face value – what do you think I should do about it?'

'Refuse to take the dogs,' responded Morfad, promptly.

'That's more easily said than done. Good relations with the Terrans are vitally important. How can I reject a warm-hearted gift without offending the givers?'

'All right, don't reject it. Modify it instead. Ask for two male or two female dogs. Make it plausible by quoting an Altairan law against the importation of alien animals that are capable of natural increase.'

'I can't do that. It's far too late. We've already accepted the animals and expressed our gratitude for them. Besides, their ability to breed is an essential part of the gift, the basic intention of the givers. They've presented us with a new species, an entire race of dogs.'

'You said it!' confirmed Morfad.

'For the same reason we can't very well prevent them from breeding when we get back home,' Haraka pointed. 'From now on we and the Terrans are going to do a lot of visiting. Immediately they discover that our dogs have failed to multiply they'll become generous and sentimental and dump another dozen on us. Or maybe a hundred. We'll then be worse off than we were before.'

'All right, all right.' Morfad shrugged with weary resignation. 'If you're going to concoct a major objection to every possible solution we may as well surrender without a fight. Let's abandon ourselves to becoming yet another dog-dominated species. Requote: to rule successfully the ruled must be unconscious of it.' He gave Haraka the sour eye. 'If I had my way, I'd wait until we were far out in free space and then give those two dogs the hearty heave-ho out the hatch.'

Haraka grinned in the manner of one about to nail down a cock-eyed tale once and for all. 'And if you did that it would be proof positive beyond all argument that you're afflicted with a delusion.'

Emitting a deep sigh, Morfad asked, 'Why would it?'

'You'd be slinging out two prime members of the master race. Some domination, eh?' Haraka grinned again. 'Listen, Morfad, according to your own story you know something never before known or suspected and you're the only one who does know it. That should make you a mighty menace to the entire species of dogs. They wouldn't let you live long enough to thwart them or even to go round advertising the truth. You'd soon be deader than a low-strata fossil.' He walked to the door, held it open while he made his parting shot. 'You look healthy enough to me.'

Morfad shouted at the closing door, 'Doesn't follow that because I can hear their thoughts they must necessarily hear mine. I doubt that they can because it's just a freakish –'

The door clicked shut. He scowled at it, walked twenty times up and down the cabin, finally resumed his chair and sat in silence while he beat his brains around in search of a satisfactory solution.

'The sharpest, most subtle, most effective weapon in the cosmos is flattery.'

Yes, he was seeking a means of coping with four-footed warriors incredibly skilled in the use of Creation's sharpest weapon. Professional fawners, creepers, worshippers, man-lovers, ego-boosters, trained to near-perfection through countless generations in an art against which there seemed no decisive defence.

How to beat off the coming attack, contain it, counter it?

'Yes, God!'

'Certainly, God!'

'Anything you say, God!'

How to protect oneself against this insidious technique, how to quarantine it or –

By the stars! that was it – *quarantine* them! On Pladamine, the useless world, the planet nobody wanted. They could breed there to their limits and meanwhile dominate the herbs and bugs. And a soothing reply would be ready for any nosy Terran tourist.

'The dogs? Oh, sure, we've still got them, lots of them. They're doing fine. Got a nice world of their very own. Place called Pladamine. If you wish to go see them, it can be arranged.'

A wonderful idea. It would solve the problem while creating no hard feelings among the Terrans. It would prove useful in the future and to the end of time. Once planted on Pladamine no dog could ever escape by its own efforts. Any tourists from Terra who brought dogs along could be persuaded to leave them in the canine heaven specially created by Altair. There the dogs would find themselves unable to boss anything higher than other dogs, and, if they didn't like it, they could lump it.

No use putting the scheme to Haraka, who was obviously prejudiced. He'd save it for the authorities back home. Even if they found it hard to credit his story, they'd still take the necessary action on the principle that it is better to be sure than sorry. Yes, they'd play safe and give Pladamine to the dogs.

Standing on a cabin seat, he gazed out and down through the port. A great mob of Terrans, far below, waited to witness the coming take-off and cheer them on their way. He noticed beyond the back of the crowd a small, absurdly groomed dog dragging a Terran female at the end of a thin, light chain. Poor girl, he thought. The dog leads, she follows yet believes *she* is taking *it* some place.

Finding his colour-camera, he checked its controls, walked along the corridor and into the open air lock. It would be nice to have a picture of the big send-off audience. Reaching the rim of the lock he tripped headlong over something four-legged and stubby-tailed that suddenly intruded itself between his feet. He dived outwards, the camera still in his grip,

and went down fast through the whistling wind while shrill feminine screams came from among the watching crowd.

Haraka said, 'The funeral has delayed us two days. We'll have to make up the time as best we can.' He brooded a moment, added, 'I am very sorry about Morfad. He had a brilliant mind but it was breaking up towards the end. Oh well, it's a comfort that the expedition has suffered only one fatality.'

'It could have been worse, sir,' responded Kashim. 'It could have been you. Praise the heavens that it was not.'

'Yes, it could have been me.' Haraka regarded him curiously. 'And would it have grieved you, Kashim?'

'Very much indeed, sir. I don't think anyone aboard would feel the loss more deeply. My respect and admiration are such that –'

He ceased as something padded softly into the cabin, laid its head in Haraka's lap, gazed soulfully up at the captain. Kashim frowned with annoyance.

'Good boy!' approved Haraka, scratching the newcomer's ears.

'My respect and admiration,' repeated Kashim in louder tones, 'are such that –'

'Good boy!' said Haraka again. He gently pulled one ear, then the other, observed with pleasure the vibrating tail.

'As I was saying, sir, my respect –'

'Good boy!' Deaf to all else, Haraka slid a hand down from the ears and massaged under the jaw.

Kashim favoured Good Boy with a glare of inutterable hatred. The dog rolled a brown eye sideways and looked at him without expression. From that moment Kashim's fate was sealed.

Harrison Bergeron
Kurt Vonnegut Jr

Kurt Vonnegut prefers not to be known as a science-fiction writer, which is odd as he has written a lot of science fiction! All his books are fascinating, and all of them are very strange. Among the best known are *The Sirens of Titan, Slaughterhouse 5, Cat's Cradle* and *Galapagos*.

There is a lot of debate in education about whether or not competition is a good thing. No competition means no losers – but if you don't have losers, you can't have winners either . . .

The year was 2081, and everybody was finally equal. They weren't only equal before God and the law. They were equal every which way. Nobody was smarter than anybody else. Nobody was better looking than anybody else. Nobody was stronger or quicker than anybody else. All this equality was due to the 211th, 212th, and 213th Amendments to the Constitution, and the unceasing vigilance of agents of the United States Handicapper General.

Some things about living still weren't quite right, though. April, for instance, still drove people crazy by not being springtime. And it was in that clammy month that the H-G men took George and Hazel Bergeron's fourteen-year-old son, Harrison, away.

It was tragic, all right, but George and Hazel couldn't think about it very hard. Hazel had a perfectly average intelligence, which meant she couldn't think about anything except in short bursts. And George, while his intelligence was way above normal, had a little mental handicap radio in his ear. He was required by law to wear it at all times. It was tuned to a government transmitter. Every 20 seconds or so, the transmitter would send out some sharp noise to keep people like George from taking unfair advantage of their brains.

George and Hazel were watching television. There were tears on Hazel's cheeks, but she'd forgotten for the moment what they were about.

On the television screen were ballerinas.

A buzzer sounded in George's head. His thoughts fled in panic, like bandits from a burglar alarm.

'That was a real pretty dance, that dance they just did,' said Hazel.

'Huh?' said George.

'That dance – it was nice,' said Hazel.

'Yup,' said George. He tried to think a little about the ballerinas. They weren't really very good – no better than anybody else would have been, anyway. They were burdened with sashweights and bags of birdshot, and their faces were masked, so that no one, seeing a free and graceful gesture or a pretty face, would feel like something the cat dragged in. George was toying with the vague notion that maybe dancers shouldn't be handicapped. But he didn't get very far with it before another noise in his ear radio scattered his thoughts.

George winced. So did two out of the eight ballerinas.

Hazel saw him wince. Having no mental handicap herself, she had to ask George what the latest sound had been.

'Sounded like somebody hitting a milk bottle with a ball peen hammer,' said George.

'I'd think it would be real interesting, hearing all the different sounds,' said Hazel, a little envious. 'All the things they think up.'

'Um,' said George.

'Only, if I was Handicapper General, you know what I would do?' said Hazel. Hazel, as a matter of fact, bore a strong resemblance to the Handicapper General, a woman named Diana Moon Glampers. 'If I was Diana Moon Glampers,' said Hazel, 'I'd have chimes on Sunday – just chimes. Kind of in honour of religion.'

'I could think, if it was just chimes,' said George.

'Well – maybe make 'em real loud,' said Hazel. 'I think I'd make a good Handicapper General.'

'Good as anybody else,' said George.

'Who knows better'n I do what normal is?' said Hazel.

'Right,' said George. He began to think glimmeringly about his abnormal son who was now in jail, about Harrison, but a twenty-one-gun salute in his head stopped that.

'Boy,' said Hazel, 'that was a doozy, wasn't it?'

It was such a doozy that George was white and trembling, and tears stood on the rims of his red eyes. Two of the eight ballerinas had collapsed to the studio floor, were holding their temples.

'All of a sudden you look so tired,' said Hazel. 'Why don't you stretch out on the sofa, so's you can rest your handicap bag on the pillows, honeybunch.' She was referring to the forty-seven pounds of birdshot in a canvas bag, which was padlocked around George's neck. 'Go and rest the bag for a little while,' she said. 'I don't care if you're not equal to me for a while.'

George weighed the bag with his hands. 'I don't mind it,' he said. 'I don't notice it any more. It's just a part of me.'

'You been so tired lately – kind of wore out,' said Hazel. 'If there was just some way we could make a little hole in the bottom of the bag, and just take out a few of them lead balls. Just a few.'

'Two years in prison and 2000 dollars fine for every ball I took out,' said George. 'I don't call that a bargain.'

'If you could just take a few out when you came home from work,' said Hazel. 'I mean – you don't compete with anybody around here. You just set around.'

'If I tried to get away with it,' said George, 'then other people'd get away with it – and pretty soon we'd be right back to the dark ages again, with everybody competing against everybody else. You wouldn't like that, would you?'

'I'd hate it,' said Hazel.

'There you are,' said George. 'The minute people start cheating on laws, what do you think happens to society?'

If Hazel hadn't been able to come up with an answer to this question, George couldn't have supplied one. A siren was going off in his head.

'Reckon it'd fall all apart,' said Hazel.

'What would?' said George blankly.

'Society,' said Hazel uncertainly. 'Wasn't that what you just said?'

'Who knows?' said George.

The television programme was suddenly interrupted for a news bulletin. It wasn't clear at first as to what the bulletin was about, since the announcer, like all announcers, had a serious speech impediment. For about half a minute, and in a state of high excitement, the announcer tried to say, 'Ladies and gentlemen –'

He finally gave up, handed the bulletin to a ballerina to read.

'That's all right –' Hazel said of the announcer, 'he tried. That's the big thing. He tried to do the best he could with what God gave him. He should get a nice raise for trying so hard.'

'Ladies and gentlemen –' said the ballerina, reading the bulletin. She must have been extraordinarily beautiful, because the mask she wore was hideous. And it was easy to see that she was the strongest and most graceful of all the dancers, for her handicap bags were as big as those worn by 200-pound men.

And she had to apologise at once for her voice, which was a very unfair voice for a woman to use. Her voice was a warm, **luminous**, timeless melody. 'Excuse me –' she said, and she began again, making her voice absolutely uncompetitive.

'Harrison Bergeron, age fourteen,' she said in a **grackle** squawk, 'has just escaped from jail, where he was held on suspicion of plotting to overthrow the government. He is a genius and an athlete, is under-handicapped, and should be regarded as extremely dangerous.'

A police photograph of Harrison Bergeron was flashed on the screen – upside down, then sideways, upside down again, then right side up. The picture showed the full length of Harrison against a background calibrated in feet and inches. He was exactly seven feet tall.

The rest of Harrison's appearance was Halloween and hardware. Nobody had ever borne heavier handicaps. He had outgrown hindrances faster than the H-G men could think them up. Instead of a little ear radio for a mental handicap, he wore a tremendous pair of earphones, and spectacles with think wavy lenses. The spectacles were intended to make him not only half blind, but to give him raging headaches besides.

Scrap metal was hung all over him. Ordinarily, there was a certain symmetry, a military neatness to the handicaps issued to strong people, but Harrison looked like a walking junkyard. In the race of life, Harrison carried 300 pounds.

And to offset his good looks, the H-G men required that he wear at all times a red rubber ball for a nose, keep his eyebrows shaved off, and cover his even white teeth with blackcaps at snaggle-tooth random.

'If you see this boy,' said the ballerina, 'do not – I repeat, do not – try to reason with him.'

There was a shriek of a door being torn from its hinges.

---

luminous: shining, bright
grackle: a mynah bird

Screams and barking cries of **consternation** came from the television set. The photograph of Harrison Bergeron on the screen jumped again and again, as though dancing to the tune of an earthquake.

George Bergeron correctly identified the earthquake, and well he might have – for many was the time his own home had danced to the same crashing tune. 'My God –' said George, 'that must be Harrison!'

The realisation was blasted from his mind instantly by the sound of an automobile collision in his head.

When George could open his eyes again, the photograph of Harrison was gone. A living, breathing Harrison filled the screen.

Clanking, clownish, and huge, Harrison stood in the centre of the studio. The knob of the uprooted studio door was still in his hand. Ballerinas, technicians, musicians, and announcers cowered on their knees before him, expecting to die.

'I am the Emperor!' cried Harrison. 'Do you hear? I am the Emperor! Everybody must do what I say at once!' He stamped his foot and the studio shook.

'Even as I stand here –' he bellowed, 'crippled, hobbled, sickened – I am a greater ruler than any man who ever lived! Now watch me become what I *can* become!'

Harrison tore the straps of his handicap harness like wet tissue paper, tore straps guaranteed to support 5000 pounds.

Harrison's scrap-iron handicaps crashed to the floor.

Harrison thrust his thumbs under the bar of the padlock that secured his head harness. The bar snapped like celery. Harrison smashed his headphones and spectacles against the wall.

He flung away his rubber-ball nose, revealed a man that would have awed Thor, the god of thunder.

---

consternation: dismay that causes confusion

'I shall now select my Empress!' he said, looking down on the cowering people. 'Let the first woman who dares rise to her feet claim her mate and her throne!'

A moment passed, and then a ballerina arose, swaying like a willow.

Harrison plucked the mental handicap from her ear, snapped off her physical handicaps with marvellous delicacy. Last of all, he removed her mask.

She was blindingly beautiful.

'Now –' said Harrison, taking her hand, 'shall we show the people the meaning of the word dance? Music!' he commanded.

The musicians scrambled back into their chairs, and Harrison stripped them of their handicaps, too. 'Play your best,' he told them, 'and I'll make you barons and dukes and earls.'

The music began. It was normal at first – cheap, silly, false. But Harrison snatched two musicians from their chairs, waved them like batons as he sang the music as he wanted it played. He slammed them back into their chairs.

The music began again and was much improved.

Harrison and his Empress merely listened to the music for a while – listened gravely, as though synchronising their heartbeats with it.

They shifted their weights to their toes.

Harrison placed his big hands on the girl's tiny waist, letting her sense the weightlessness that would soon be hers.

And then, in an explosion of joy and grace, into the air they sprang!

Not only were the laws of the land abandoned, but the law of gravity and the laws of motion as well.

They reeled, whirled, swivelled, flounced, capered, gambolled, and spun.

They leaped like deer on the moon.

The studio ceiling was 30 feet high, but each leap brought the dancers nearer to it.

It became their obvious intention to kiss the ceiling.

They kissed it.

And then, neutralising gravity with love and pure will, they remained suspended in air inches below the ceiling, and they kissed each other for a long, long time.

It was then that Diana Moon Glampers, the Handicapper General, came into the studio with a double-barrelled ten-gauge shotgun. She fired twice, and the Emperor and the Empress were dead before they hit the floor.

Diana Moon Glampers loaded the gun again. She aimed it at the musicians and told them they had ten seconds to get their handicaps back on.

It was then that the Bergerons' television tube burned out.

Hazel turned to comment about the blackout to George. But George had gone out into the kitchen for a can of beer.

George came back in with the beer, paused while a handicap signal shook him up. And then he sat down again. 'You been crying?' he said to Hazel.

'Yup,' she said.

'What about?' he said.

'I forget,' she said. 'Something real sad on television.'

'What was it?' he said.

'It's all kind of mixed up in my mind,' said Hazel.

'Forget sad things,' said George.

'I always do,' said Hazel.

'That's my girl,' said George. He winced. There was the sound of a rivetting gun in his head.

'Gee – I could tell that one was a doozy,' said Hazel.

'You can say that again,' said George.

'Gee –' said Hazel, 'I could tell that one was a doozy.'

At Last, The True
Story of Frankenstein
Harry Harrison

There are very few writers who can have you crying with laughter one minute and hiding under the bedclothes, quaking with fear, the next. Harry Harrison is one of those writers.

His space opera spoofs, *Bill the Galactic Hero* and the *Stainless Steel Rat* series, are among the funniest books in science fiction. But he also enjoys freezing the blood. His novel *Make Room! Make Room!* was made into the film *Soylent Green*. And if you won't know what Soylent Green is, we're certainly not going to tell you. And while we're on the subject of horror, here's a tale to keep you awake at night . . .

'Und here, before your very eyes, is the very same monster built by my much admired great-great-grandfather, Victor Frankenstein, built by him from pieces of corpses out of the dissecting rooms, stolen parts of bodies freshly buried in the grave, und even chunks of animals from the slaughterhouse. Now look –' The tall-coated man on the platform swung his arm out in a theatrical gesture and the heads of the close-packed crowd below swung to follow it. The dusty curtains flapped aside and the monster stood there, illuminated from above by a sickly green light. There was a concerted gasp from the crowd and a shiver of motion.

In the front row, pressed against the rope barrier, Dan Bream mopped his face with a soggy handkerchief and smiled. It wasn't such a bad monster, considering that this was a cheapjack carnival playing the smalltown southern circuit. It had a dead-white skin, undampened by sweat even in this steambath of a tent, glazed eyes, stitches and seams showing where the face had been patched together, and the two metal plugs projecting from the temples – just like in the movie.

'Raise your right arm!' Victor Frankenstein V commanded, his brusque German accent giving the words a Prussian air of authority. The monster's body did not move, but slowly – with the jerking motion of a badly operating machine – the creature's arm came up to shoulder height and stopped.

'This monster, built from pieces from the dead, cannot die, und if a piece gets too worn out I simply stitch on a new piece with the secret formula passed down from father to son from my great-great-grandfather. It cannot die nor feel pain – as you see –'

This time the gasp was even louder and some of the audience turned away while others watched with eager eyes. The barker had taken a foot-long and wickedly sharp needle, and had pushed it firmly through the monster's biceps until it protruded on both sides. No blood stained it and the creature made no motion, as though completely unaware that anything had been done to its flesh.

' . . . **impervious** to pain, extremes of heat and cold, and possessing the strength of ten men . . .'

Behind him the voice droned on, but Dan Bream had had enough. He had seen the performance three times before, which was more than satisfactory for what he needed to know, and if he stayed in the tent another minute he would melt. The exit was close by and he pushed through the gaping, **pallid** audience and out into the humid dusk. It wasn't much cooler outside. Life

---

impervious: not responsive to
pallid: pale

borders on the unbearable along the shores of the Gulf of Mexico in August, and Panama City, Florida, was no exception. Dan headed for the nearest air-conditioned beer joint and sighed with relief as the chill atmosphere closed around his steaming garments. The beer bottle frosted instantly with condensation as did the heavy glass **stein**, cold from the freezer. The first big swallow cut a path straight down to his stomach. He took the beer over to one of the straight-backed wooden booths, wiped the table off with a handful of paper napkins and flopped onto the bench. From the inner pocket of his jacket he took some folded sheets of yellow copy paper, now slightly soggy, and spread them before him. After adding some lines to the scribbled notes he stuffed them back into his jacket and took a long pull on his beer.

Dan was halfway through his second bottle when the barker, who called himself Frankenstein the Fifth, came in. His stage personality had vanished along with the **frock coat** and a monocle, and the Prussian haircut now looked like a common crewcut.

'You've got a great act,' Dan called out cheerfully, and waved the man over. 'Will you join me for a drink?'

'Don't mind if I do,' Frankenstein answered in the pure nasal vowels of New York City, the German accent apparently having disappeared along with the monocle. 'And see if they have a Schlitz or a Bud or anything beside the local swamp water.'

He settled into the booth while Dan went for the beers, and groaned when he saw the labels on the bottles.

'At least it's cold,' he said, shaking salt into his to make it foam, then half drained the stein in a long deep swallow. 'I noticed you out there in front of the **clems** for

---

stein: a large beer mug
frock coat: a man's long-skirted coat
clems: punters

most of the shows today. Do you like the act – or you a **carny buff?**''

'It's a good act. I'm a newsman, name's Dan Bream.'

'Always pleased to meet the Press, Dan. Publicity is the life of show business, as the man said. I'm Stanley Arnold: call me Stan.'

'Then Frankenstein is just your stage name?'

'What else? You act kinda dim for a reporter, are you sure –?' He waved away the Press card that Dan pulled from his breast pocket. 'No, I believe you, Dan, but you gotta admit the question was **a little on the rube side**. I bet you even think that I have a real monster in there!'

'Well, you must admit that he looks authentic. The skin stitched together that way, those plugs in his head –'

'Held on with spirit gum and the embroidery is drawn on with eyebrow pencil. That's show business for you, all illusion. But I'm happy to hear that the act even looked real to an experienced reporter like yourself. What paper did you say you were with?'

'No paper, the news syndicate. I caught your act about six months ago and became interested. Did a little checking when I was in Washington, then followed you down here. You don't really want me to call you Stan, do you? Stein might be closer. After all – Victor Frankenstein *is* the name on your naturalisation papers.'

'Tell me more,' Frankenstein said in a voice suddenly cold and emotionless.

Dan rifled through the yellow sheets. 'Yes . . . here it is, from the official records. Frankenstein, Victor – born in Geneva, arrived in the US in 1938, and more of the same.'

'The next thing you'll be telling me is that my monster *is* real!' Frankenstein smiled, but only with his mouth.

'I'm betting that it is. No yogi training or hypnotism or

---

carny buff: a fan of carnival
a little on the rube side: a bit on the daft side

such can make a man as indifferent to pain as that thing is – and as terribly strong. I want the whole story, the truth for a change!'

'Do you . . .?' Frankenstein asked in a cold voice and for a long moment the air filled with tension. Then he laughed and clapped the reporter on the arm. 'All right, Dan – I'll give it to you. You are a persistent devil and a good reporter and it is the least you deserve. But first you must get us some more drinks, something a measurable degree stronger than this **execrable** beer.' His New York accent had disappeared as easily as had his German one; he spoke English now with skill and perfection without any recognisable regional accent.

Dan gathered their empty glasses. 'It'll have to be beer – this is a dry county.'

'Nonsense! This is America, the land that raises its hands in horror at the foreign conception of double-think yet practises it with an efficiency that sets the Old World to shame. Bay County may be officially dry but the law has many itchy palms, and under that counter you will find a reasonable supply of a clear liquid that glories in the name of White Mule and is reputed to have a kick of the same magnitude as its **cognate** beast. If you are still in doubt you will see a framed federal liquor licence on the far wall, legitimising this endeavour in the eyes of the national government. Simply place a five-dollar banknote on the bar, say Mountain Dew, and do not expect any change.'

When they both had enjoyed their first sips of the corn liquor Victor Frankenstein lapsed into a friendly mood.

'Call me Vic, Dan. I want us to be friends. I'm going to tell you a story that few have heard before, a story that is astounding but true. True – mark that word – not

---

cognate: of the same name
execrable: very bad

a hodge-podge of distortions and half-truths and outright ignorance like that vile book produced by Mary Godwin. Oh how my father ever regretted meeting that woman and, in a moment of weakness, confiding in her the secret of some of his original lines of research . . .'

'Just a minute,' Dan broke in. 'You mentioned the truth, but I can't swallow this guff. Mary Wollstonecraft Shelley wrote *Frankenstein; or, The Modern Prometheus* in 1818. Which would make you and your father so old . . .'

'Please, Dan – no interruptions. I mentioned my father's researches, in the plural you will note, all of them devoted to the secrets of life. The Monster, as it has come to be called, was just one of his works. Longevity was what he was interested in, and he did live to a very, very old age, as will I. I will not stretch your **credulity** any further at this moment by mentioning the year of my birth, but will press on. That Mary Godwin. She and the poet were living together at this period, they had not married as yet, and this permitted my father to hope that Mary might one day find him not unattractive, since he was quite taken by her. Well, you can easily imagine the end. She made notes of everything he told her – then **discarded** him and used the notes to construct her **despicable** book. Her errors are legion, listen . . .' He leaned across the booth and once again clapped Dan on the shoulder in a hearty way. It was an intimate gesture that the reporter didn't particularly enjoy, but he didn't complain. Not as long as the other kept talking.

'Firstly she made papa a Swiss; he used to tear his hair out at the thought, since ours is a good old Bavarian family with a noble and ancient lineage. Then she had

---

credulity: ability to believe
discarded: threw away
despicable: disgraceful

him attending the University of Ingolstadt in *Ingolstadt* – when every schoolboy knows that it was moved to Landshut in 1800. And father's personality, what crimes she committed there! In this libellous volume he is depicted as a weeping and ineffectual man, when in reality he was a tower of strength and determination. And if this isn't enough, she completely misunderstood the meaning of his experiments. Her **gimcrack** collection of cast-off parts put together to make an artificial man is **ludicrous**. She was so carried away by the legends of Talos and the Golem that she misinterpreted my father's work and cast it into that ancient mould. Father did not construct an artificial man, he reactivated a *dead* man! That is the measure of his genius! He travelled for years in the darkest reaches of the African jungle, learning the lore of the creation of the zombie. He regularised the knowledge and improved upon it until he had surpassed all of his aboriginal teachers. Raise the dead, that is what he could do. That was his secret – and how can it be kept a secret in the future, Mr Dan Bream?'

With these last words Victor Frankenstein's eyes opened wide and an unveiled light seemed to glow in their depths. Dan pulled back instinctively, then relaxed. He was in no danger here in this brightly lit room with men on all sides of them.

'Afraid, Dan? Don't be.' Victor smiled and reached out and patted Dan on the shoulder once again.

'What was that?' Dan asked, startled at the tiny brief pain in his shoulder.

'Nothing – nothing but this,' Frankenstein smiled again, but the smile had changed subtly and no longer contained any humour. He opened his hand to reveal a small

---

gimcrack: worthless
ludicrous: ridiculous

hypodermic needle, its plunger pushed down and its barrel empty.

'Remain seated,' he said quietly when Dan started to rise, and Dan's muscles relaxed and he sat back down, horrified.

'What have you done to me?'

'Very little – the injection is harmless. A simple little hypnotic drug, the effect of which wears off in a few hours. But until then you will not have much will of your own. So you will sit and hear me out. Drink some beer though, we don't want you to be thirsty.'

Horrified, Dan was a helpless onlooker as, of its own volition, his hand raised and poured a measure of beer down his throat.

'Now concentrate, Dan, think of the significance of my statement. The so-called Frankenstein monster is no stitched-up collection of scraps, but a good honest zombie. A dead man who can walk but not talk, obey but not think. **Animate** – but still dead. Poor old Charley is one, the creature whom you watched going through his act on the platform. But Charley is just about worn out. Since he is dead he cannot replace the body cells that are destroyed during the normal wear and tear of the day. Why the fellow is like an animated pincushion from the act, holes everywhere. His feet – terrible, not a toe left, keep breaking off when he walks too fast. I think it's time to retire Charley. He has had a long life, and a long death. Stand up, Dan.'

In spite of his mind crying *No! No!* Dan rose slowly to his feet.

'Aren't you interested in what Charley used to do before he became a sideshow monster? You should be, Dan. Old Charley was a reporter – just like you. And he ran across what he thought was a good story. Like

---

animate: able to move

you, he didn't realise the importance of what he had discovered and talked to me about it. You reporters are a very inquisitive bunch. I must show you my scrapbook, it's simply filled with Press cards. Before you die of course. You wouldn't be able to appreciate it afterwards. Now come along.'

Dan walked after him, into the hot night, screaming inside a haze of terror, yet walking quietly and silently down the street.

The Tunnel of Love
Robert Bloch

Robert Bloch is one of the most versatile writers around, so it seems unfair that he also happens to be one of the best. He's written everything from episodes of *Star Trek* (*'What Are Little Girls Made Of?'*, *'Catspaw'* and *'Wolf in the Fold'* from the original series, if you must know) to the Alfred Hitchcock film *Psycho*.

Like Ray Bradbury, he's equally at home in sci-fi, fantasy and horror. This little gore-fest is one of his finest. Enjoy!

The entrance to the tunnel had been painted to resemble a woman's mouth, with Cupid's-bow lips bordering it in vivid red. Marco stared into the yawning darkness beyond. A woman's mouth – how often had he dreamed of it, this past winter?

Now he stood before the entrance, stood before the mouth, waiting to be engulfed.

Marco was all alone in the amusement park; none of the other **concessionaires** had come to inspect their property and put it in working order for the new season. He was all alone, standing before the mouth; the scarlet mouth that beckoned him to come, be swallowed, be devoured.

It would be so easy to run away, clear out and never come back. Maybe when the summer season opened he could sell the concession. He'd tried all winter long, but there'd been no takers, even at a ridiculously low price. Yes, he could sell out and go away, far away. Away from the

---

concessionaires: the people who hold the right to trade, i.e. the other stallholders in the amusement park

tunnel, away from the red mouth with its black throat gaping for some human morsels.

But that was nonsense, dream-stuff, nightmare. The Tunnel of Love was a good stand, a money-maker. A four-months' take was enough to support him for an entire year. And he needed the money, needed it more than ever since he'd married Dolores.

Perhaps he shouldn't have married her, in view of his troubles, but in a way that's just why he had to marry her. He wanted something to cling to, something to shut out the fears that came to him at night. She loved him, and she would never suspect; there was no need for her to suspect if he kept his own head. Everything was going to be all right once the season started. Now all he needed to do was check up on his equipment.

The ticket booth was in good shape; he'd opened it and found no damage through leaking or frost. A good coat of paint would help, and he'd put a new stool inside for Dolores. She'd sell the tickets next season and cut down on his overhead. All he need bother about would be running the boats through; shoving them off and docking them for the benefit of the giggling couples who eagerly tasted the delights of the Tunnel of Love.

Marco had checked the six gondolas stored in the shed behind the boards fronting his concession. All were sound. The treadmill motor was oiled and ready. The water intake and outlet were unrusted. He had dragged one of the flat-bottomed gondolas out and it lay ready for launching once he flooded the channel and started the treadmill operation.

Now he hesitated before the tunnel entrance. This was it. He had to make up his mind, once and for all. Would he . . .

Turning his back deliberately on the jaws of the monster (he had to stop thinking like that, he *had* to!) Marco stepped over and opened the water. It ran down into the channel, a thin brown trickle, a muddy jet, a gushing frothy stream. The tunnel swallowed it. Now the treadmill was obscured; the water rushed into the tunnel full force. It rose as it flowed until the normal depth of three feet was attained. Marco watched it pour into the mouth. The mouth was thirsty. Thirsty for water, thirsty for . . .

Marco closed his eyes. If only he could get rid of that crazy notion about mouths! Funny thing, the exit of the tunnel didn't bother him at all. The exit was just as big, just as black. The water would rush through the entrance, complete the circuit of the tunnel, and emerge on the other side from the exit. It would sweep over the dry treadmill, clean out the dirt and the debris, the accumulation of past months. It would sweep it out clean, bring everything from the tunnel, it was coming now, yes, he could hear it now; he wanted to run, he couldn't look!

But Marco had to look. He had to know. He had to find out what floated on that bubbling, gurgling stream; had to see what bobbed and twisted in the torrent that emerged from the tunnel exit.

The water trickled, eddied, churned, swept out in a raging and majestic tide. Marco knelt in the gutter and stared down at the flow. It would be a haemorrhage, it would be blood, he knew that; but how could it be? Marco stared and saw that it wasn't blood. Nothing emerged from the tunnel but dirty water – dirty water carrying caravels of leaves, a fleet of twigs, a flotilla of old gum-wrappers and cigarette butts. The surface of the water was rainbow-veined with oil and grease. It eddied and mingled once again with the steady flow from the faucets leading back into the tunnel. The level rose to the markings on the side of the **treadle**-pit.

So the tunnel was empty. Marco sighed gratefully. It had all been a nightmare; his fears were groundless. Now

---

treadle: a paddle that sends water flowing through the tunnel all he needed to do was launch the single gondola and go through the tunnel for an inspection of the lights on his exhibits.

Yes, all he had to do was sail into the waiting mouth, the hungry mouth, the grinning jaws of death –

Marco shrugged, shook his head. No use stalling, he had to go through with it. He'd turn the lights on; he could use the handswitches en route to stop the treadle if needs be. Then he could inspect the cut-off and see if everything was barricaded off. There was nothing to worry about, but he had to be quite *sure*.

He slid the heavy gondola off its truck and into the channel. Holding it with a boat-hook, he stooped again and switched on the motor. It chugged. The treadle groaned under the water, and he knew it was moving. The deep, flat-bottomed gondola rested on the moving treadle struts. Marco let the boat-hook fall and stepped into the forward seat of the boat. It began to move forward, move towards the red lips, the black mouth. The entrance of the tunnel loomed.

Marco leaped from the boat with a spastic, convulsive tremour agitating his limbs. Frantically, he switched off the motor and halted the gondola at the lip of the tunnel. He stood there, all panting and perspiration, for a long moment.

Thank God, he'd thought of it in time! He'd almost gone into the tunnel without remembering to turn on the lights. That he could never do, he knew; the lights were necessary. How could he have forgotten? *Why* had he forgotten? Did the tunnel want him to forget? Did it want him to go into the blackness all alone, so that it could . . .

Marco shook his head. Such thoughts were childish. Quite deliberately, he walked into the ticket booth and plugged in the cord controlling the tunnel light circuit.

He started the treadle going and jumped into the moving boat, barking his left shin. He was still rubbing the sore spot as the boat glided into darkness.

Quite suddenly Marco was in the tunnel, and he wasn't afraid any more. There was nothing to be afraid of, nothing at all. The boat bumped along slowly, the water gurgled, the treadle groaned. Little blue lights cast a friendly glow at intervals of 40 feet – little blue lights behind the glass walls of the small papier-mâché exhibit booths set in the tunnel sides. Here was Romeo and Juliet, here was Antony and Cleopatra, here was Napoleon and Josephine, here was the cut-out . . .

Marco stopped the boat – halted the treadle, rather, by reaching out and pulling the handswitch set near the water's edge in the left wall of the tunnel.

Here was the cut-out . . .

Formerly the tunnel had contained an extra loop; 120 feet more of winding channel through which boats had doubled back on an auxiliary treadle. Since November this channel had been cut out, boarded up, sealed up tightly and cemented at the cracks by Marco's frantic fingers. He had worked until after midnight to do the job, but it was well done. Marco stared at the wall. It had held. Nothing leaked into the cut-out, nothing leaked out of it. The air of the tunnel was **foetid**, but that was merely a natural musty odour soon to be dispelled – just as Marco's fears were dispelled now by the sight of the smooth walled surface.

There was nothing to worry about, nothing at all. Marco started the treadle. The boat swept on. Now he could lean back in his double seat and actually enjoy the ride. The Tunnel of Love would operate again. The **bobby-soxers** and the college kids, the sailors

---

foetid: stinking
bobby-soxer: adolescent girl

and the **hicks** would have their romance, their smooching, their dime's-worth of darkness. Yes, Marco would sell darkness for a dime. He lived on darkness. He and Dolores would be together; just like Romeo and Juliet, Antony and Cleopatra, Marco and – but *that* was over.

Marco was actually grinning when the boat glided out into the light of day again.

Dolores saw the grin and thought it was meant for her. She waved from the side of the channel.

'Hello, darling!'

Marco gaped at the tall blonde in the flowered print dress. She waved at him, and as the boat drew up opposite the disembarking point she stooped, stopped the motor, and held out her arms to the man in the gondola. His grin disappeared as he rose.

'What are you doing here?'

'Just thought I'd surprise you. I guessed where you'd be going.' Her arms pressed his back.

'Oh.' He kissed her without giving or receiving any sensation.

'You aren't mad, are you, darling? After all, I'm your wife – and I'm going to be working here with you, aren't I? I mean, I'd like to see this old tunnel you've been so mysterious about.'

Lord, she was a stupid female! Maybe that's why he loved her; because she was stupid, and uncalculating, and loyal. Because she wasn't dark and intense and knowing and hysterical like . . .

'What on earth were you doing?' she asked.

The question threw him off balance. 'Why, just going through the tunnel.'

'All alone?' Dolores giggled. 'What's the sense of taking a boat ride through the Tunnel of Love by yourself? Couldn't you find some girl to keep you company?'

---

hick: countryman

If you only knew, thought Marco, but he didn't say it. He didn't care. 'Just inspecting the place,' he said. 'Seems to be in good shape. Shall we go now?'

'Go?' Dolores pouted. 'I want to see, too.'

'There's nothing to see.'

'Come on, darling – take me through the tunnel, just once. After all, I won't be getting a chance after the season opens.'

'But . . .'

She teased his hair with her fingers. 'Look, I drove all the way down here just to see. What're you acting so mysterious about? You hiding a body in the tunnel, or something?'

Good Lord, not that, Marco thought. He couldn't allow her to become suspicious.

Not Dolores, of all people.

'You really want to go through?' he murmured. He knew she did, and he knew he had to take her, now. He had to show her that there was nothing to be afraid of, there was nothing in the tunnel at all.

And why couldn't he do just that? There *was* nothing to fear, nothing at all. So – 'Come along,' said Marco.

He helped her into the boat, holding the gondola steady in the swirling water as he started the treadle. Then he jumped into the seat beside her and cast off. The boat bumped against the sides of the channel and swayed as he sat down. She gasped.

'Be careful or we'll tip!' she squealed.

'Not a chance. This outfit's safe. Besides, the water's only three feet deep at most. You can't get hurt here.'

Oh, can't you? Marco wiped his forehead and grimaced as the gondola edged towards the gulping black hole of the Tunnel of Love. He buried his face against her cheek and closed his eyes against the engulfing darkness.

'Gee, honey, isn't it romantic?' Dolores whispered. 'I bet you used to envy the fellows who took their girls through here, didn't you? Or did you get girls and go through yourself?'

Marco wished she'd shut up. This kind of talk he didn't like to hear.

'Did you ever take that girl you used to have in the ticket booth in here with you?' Dolores teased. 'What was her name – Belle?'

'No,' said Marco.

'What did you say happened to her at the end of the season, darling?'

'She ran out on me.' Marco kept his head down, his eyes closed. They were in the tunnel now and he could smell the mustiness of it. It smelled like old perfume – stale, cheap perfume. He knew that smell. He pressed his face against Dolores's cheek. She wore scent, but the other smell still came through.

'I never liked her,' Dolores was saying. 'What kind of a girl was she, Marco? I mean, did you ever . . .'

'No – no!'

'Well, don't snap at me like that! I've never seen you act like this before, Marco.'

'*Marco.*' The name echoed through the tunnel. It bounced off the ceiling, off the walls, off the cut-out. It echoed and re-echoed, and then it was taken up from far away in a different voice; a softer voice, gurgling through water. *Marco, Marco, Marco*, over and over again until he couldn't stand it.

'Shut up!' yelled Marco.

'Why . . .'

'Not you, Dolores. Her.'

'Her? Are you nuts or something? There's nobody but the two of us here in the dark, and . . .'

In the dark? How could that be? The lights were on, he'd left them on. What was she talking about?

Marco opened his eyes. They *were* in the dark. The lights were out. Perhaps a fuse had blown. Perhaps a short circuit.

There was no time to think of possibilities. All Marco knew was the certainty; they were gliding down the dark throat of the tunnel in the dark, nearing the centre, nearing the cut-out. And the echo, the damned drowned echo, whispered, '*Marco.*'

He had to shut it out, he had to talk over it, talk against it. And all at once he was talking, fast and shrill.

'She did it, Dolores, I know she did it. Belle. She's here now, in the tunnel. All winter long I felt her, saw her, heard her in my dreams. Calling to me. Calling to me to come back. She said I'd never be rid of her, you'd never have me, nobody and nothing could take me away from her. And I was a fool – I came back, I let you come with me. Now we're here and she's here. Can't you feel it?'

'Darling.' She clung to him in the dark. 'You're not well, are you? Because there's nobody here. You understand that, don't you? Belle ran away, remember, you told me yourself. She's not here.'

'Oh yes she is!' Marco panted. 'She's here, she's been here all along, ever since last season. She died in this tunnel.'

Dolores wasn't clinging to him any more. She drew away. The boat rocked and bumped the channel sides. He couldn't see anything in the perfumed blackness, and he had to get her arms around him again. So he talked faster.

'She died here. The night we took a ride together after I closed the concession. The night I told her I was going to marry you, that it was all over between her and me. She jumped out of the boat and tried to take me with her. I guess I fought her.

'Belle was hysterical, you must understand that. She kept saying it over and over again, that I couldn't leave her, that she'd never give me up, never. I tried to pull her back into the boat and she choked me and then she – drowned.'

'You killed her!'

'I didn't. It was an accident, suicide, really. I didn't mean to hold her so tight but she was fighting me – it was just suicide. I knew it looked like murder, I knew what would happen if anyone found out. So I buried her, walled her up behind the cut-out. And now she's coming back, she won't let me go, what shall I do, Dolores, what can I do?'

'You . . .'

Dolores screamed.

Marco tried to put his arms around her. She moved away, shrieking. The echo shattered the darkness. He lunged at her. The boat rocked and tipped. There was a splash.

'Come back, you fool!' Marco stood up, groping in darkness. Somewhere Dolores was wailing and gurgling. The gondola was empty now. The blackness was spinning round and round, sucking Marco down into it. He felt a bump, knew the boat had stopped. He jumped out into the water. The treadles were slippery with slime. Cold waves lapped about his waist. He tried to find Dolores in the darkness, in the water. No wailing now, no gurgles.

'Dolores!'

No answer. No sound at all. The bumping and the lapping ceased.

'Dolores!'

She hadn't run away. There was nowhere to run to, and he would have heard the splashing. Then she was . . .

His hands found flesh. Wet flesh, floating flesh. She had fallen against the side of the boat, bumped her head. But only a few seconds had passed. Nobody drowns in a few seconds. She had passed out, poor kid.

He dragged her into the boat. Now it moved away, moved through the darkness as he propped her on the seat beside him and put his arm around the clammy, soggy wetness of her dress. Her head lolled on his shoulder as he chafed her wrists.

'There, now. It's all right. Don't you see, darling, it's all right now? I'm not afraid any more. Belle isn't here. There's nothing to worry about. Everything will be all right.'

The more he said it, the more he knew it was true. What had he done, frightening the girl half to death? Marco cursed the slowness of the treadles as the boat bumped its way out of the tunnel. The mechanism wasn't working properly. But there was no time to bother about that. He had to bring Dolores around.

He kissed her hair. He kissed her ear. She was still cold. 'Come on, honey,' he whispered. 'Brace up. This is the Tunnel of Love, remember?'

The boat bumped out into the daylight. Marco stared ahead. They were safe now. Safe from the tunnel, safe from Belle. He and Dolores . . .

Dolores.

Marco peered at the prow of the bumping gondola as it creaked over the treadles. He peered at the obstruction floating in its path; floating face upward in the water as if tied to the boat with a red string running from its gashed forehead.

Dolores!

She had fallen in the water when she jumped out of the gondola, fallen and struck her head the way Belle had struck her head. It was Dolores's body that bumped against the front of the boat and retarded its progress. She was dead.

But if that was Dolores out there in the water, then what . . .

Marco turned his head, ever so slowly. For the first time he glanced down at the seat beside him, at what lay cradled in his arms.

For the first time Marco saw what he had been kissing . . .

. . . the boat glided back into the Tunnel of Love.

We Can Remember It
For You Wholesale

Philip K. Dick

Few science-fiction writers have been well served by Hollywood. Philip K. Dick is an exception. His novel *Do Androids Dream of Electric Sheep?* was made into one of sci-fi's film masterpieces: *Blade Runner,* starring Harrison Ford. His other books include *Flow My Tears The Policeman Said* and *The World Jones Made*.

This story was also the inspiration for a film – the Arnold Schwarzenegger blockbuster, *Total Recall*.

He awoke – and wanted Mars. The valleys, he thought. What would it be like to trudge among them? Great and greater yet: the dream grew as he became fully conscious, the dream and the yearning. He could almost feel the enveloping presence of the other world, which only government agents and high officials had seen. A clerk like himself? Not likely.

'Are you getting up or not?' his wife Kirsten asked drowsily, with her usual hint of fierce crossness. 'If you are, push the hot coffee button on the darn stove.'

'Okay,' Douglas Quail said, and made his way barefoot from the bedroom of their conapt to the kitchen. There, having dutifully pressed the hot coffee button, he seated himself at the kitchen table, brought out a yellow, small tin of fine Dean Swift snuff. He inhaled briskly, and the Beau Nash mixture stung his nose, burned the roof of his mouth. But still he inhaled; it woke him up and allowed his dreams, his nocturnal desires and random wishes, to condense into a semblance of rationality.

I will go, he said to himself. *Before I die I'll see Mars.*

It was, of course, impossible, and he knew this even as he dreamed. But the daylight, the **mundane** noise of his wife now brushing her hair before the bedroom mirror – everything conspired to remind him of what he was. *A miserable little salaried employee*, he said to himself with bitterness. Kirsten reminded him of this at least once a day and he did not blame her; it was a wife's job to bring her husband down to Earth. *Down to Earth*, he thought, and laughed. The figure of speech in this was literally apt.

'What are you sniggering about?' his wife asked as she swept into the kitchen, her long busy-pink robe wagging after her. 'A dream, I bet. You're always full of them.'

'Yes,' he said, and gazed out the kitchen window at the hovercars and traffic runnels, and all the little energetic people hurrying to work. In a little while he would be among them. As always.

'I'll bet it has to do with some woman,' Kirsten said witheringly.

'No,' he said. 'A god. The god of war. He has wonderful craters with every kind of plant-life growing deep down in them.'

'Listen.' Kirsten crouched down beside him and spoke earnestly, the harsh quality momentarily gone from her voice. 'The bottom of the ocean – *our* ocean is much more, an infinity of times more beautiful. You know that; everyone knows that. Rent an artificial gill-outfit for both of us, take a week off from work, and we can descend and live down there at one of those year-round aquatic resorts. And in addition –' She broke off. 'You're not listening. You should be. Here is something a lot better than that compulsion, that obsession you have about Mars, and you don't even listen!' Her voice rose piercingly. 'God in heaven, you're doomed, Doug! What's going to become of you?'

---

mundane: ordinary, everyday

'I'm going to work,' he said, rising to his feet, his breakfast forgotten. 'That's what's going to become of me.'

She eyed him. 'You're getting worse. More fanatical every day. Where's it going to lead?'

'To Mars,' he said, and opened the door to the closet to get down a fresh shirt to wear to work.

Having descended from the taxi Quail slowly walked across three densely-populated foot runnels and to the modern, attractively inviting doorway. There he halted, impeding mid-morning traffic, and with caution read the shifting-colour neon sign. He had, in the past, scrutinised this sign before . . . but never had he come so close. This was very different; what he did now was something else. Something which sooner or later had to happen.

REKAL, INCORPORATED

Was this the answer? After all, an illusion, no matter how convincing, remained nothing more than an illusion. At least objectively. But **subjectively** – quite the opposite entirely.

And anyhow he had an appointment. Within the next five minutes.

Taking a deep breath of mildly smog-infested Chicago air, he walked through the dazzling **polychromatic** shimmer of the doorway and up to the receptionist's counter.

The **nicely-articulated** blonde at the counter, bare-bosomed and tidy, said pleasantly, 'Good morning, Mr Quail.'

---

subjectively: from the point of view of one's feelings rather than what actually exists

polychromatic: multi-coloured

nicely-articulated: well-spoken

'Yes,' he said. 'I'm here to see about a Rekal course. As I guess you know.'

'Not "rekal" but *re*call,' the receptionist corrected him. She picked up the receiver of the vidphone by her smooth elbow and said into it, 'Mr Douglas Quail is here, Mr McClane. May he come inside, now? Or is it too soon?'

'Giz wetwa wum-wum wamp,' the phone mumbled.

'Yes, Mr Quail,' she said. 'You may go in; Mr McClane is expecting you.' As he started off uncertainly she called after him, 'Room D, Mr Quail. To your right.'

After a frustrating but brief moment of being lost he found the proper room. The door hung open and inside, at a big genuine walnut desk, sat a genial-looking man, middle-aged, wearing the latest Martian frog-pelt grey suit; his attire alone would have told Quail that he had come to the right person.

'Sit down, Douglas,' McClane said, waving his plump hand towards a chair which faced the desk. 'So you want to have gone to Mars. Very good.'

Quail seated himself, feeling tense. 'I'm not so sure this is worth the fee,' he said. 'It costs a lot and as far as I can see I really get nothing.' *Costs almost as much as going*, he thought.

'You get tangible proof of your trip,' McClane disagreed emphatically. 'All the proof you'll need. Here; I'll show you.' He dug within a drawer of his impressive desk. 'Ticket stub.' Reaching into a **manila** folder, he produced a small square of embossed cardboard. 'It proves you went – and returned. Postcards.' He laid out four franked picture 3-D full-colour postcards in a neatly-arranged row on the desk for Quail to see. 'Film. Shots you took of local sights on Mars with a rented moving camera.' To Quail he displayed those, too. 'Plus the names of people you met, 200 poscreds worth of souvenirs, which will arrive – from Mars – within the following month. And passport, certificates listing the shots you received. And more.' He glanced up keenly at Quail. 'You'll know you went, all right,' he said. 'You won't remember us, won't remember me or ever having been here. It'll be a real trip in your mind; we guarantee that. A full two weeks of recall; every last piddling detail. Remember this: if at any time you doubt that you really took an extensive trip to Mars you can return here and get a full refund. You see?'

'But I didn't go,' Quail said. 'I won't have gone, no matter what proofs you provide me with.' He took a deep, unsteady breath. 'And I never was a secret agent with Interplan.' It seemed impossible to him that Rekal, Incorporated's extra-factual memory implant would do its job – despite what he had heard people say.

---

manila: strong (brown) paper

'Mr Quail,' McClane said patiently. 'As you explained in your letter to us, you have no chance, no possibility in the slightest, of ever actually getting to Mars; you can't afford it, and what is much more important, you could never qualify as an undercover agent for Interplan or anybody else. This is the only way you can achieve your, ahem, life-long dream; am I not correct, sir? You can't be this; you can't actually do this.' He chuckled. 'But you can *have been* and *have done*. We see to that. And our fee is reasonable; no hidden charges.' He smiled encouragingly.

'Is an extra-factual memory that convincing?' Quail asked.

'More than the real thing, sir. Had you really gone to Mars as an Interplan agent, you would by now have forgotten a great deal; our analysis of true-mem systems – authentic recollections of major events in a person's life – shows that a variety of details are very quickly lost to the person. Forever. Part of the package we offer you is such deep implantation of recall that nothing is forgotten. The packet which is fed to you while you're comatose is the creation of trained experts, men who have spent years on Mars; in every case we verify details down to the last iota. And you've picked a rather easy extra-factual system; had you picked Pluto or wanted to be Emperor of the Inner Planet Alliance we'd have much more difficulty . . . and the charges would be considerably greater.'

Reaching into his coat for his wallet, Quail said, 'Okay. It's been my life-long ambition and so I see I'll never really do it. So I guess I'll have to settle for this.'

'Don't think of it that way,' McClane said severely. 'You're not accepting second-best. The actual memory, with all its vagueness, omissions and ellipses, not to say distortions – that's second-best.' He accepted the money and pressed a button on his desk. 'All right, Mr Quail,' he said, as the door of his office opened and two burly men swiftly entered. 'You're on your way to Mars as a secret agent.' He rose, came over to shake Quail's nervous, moist hand. 'Or rather, you have been on your way. This afternoon at four-thirty you will, um, arrive back here on Terra; a cab will leave you off at your conapt and as I say you will never remember seeing me or coming here; you won't, in fact, even remember having heard of our existence.'

His mouth dry with nervousness, Quail followed the two technicians from the office; what happened next depended on them.

Will I actually believe I've been on Mars? he wondered. *That I managed to fulfil my lifetime ambition?* He had a strange, lingering intuition that something would go wrong. But just what – he did not know.

He would have to wait to find out.

The intercom on McClane's desk, which connected him with the work-area of the firm, buzzed and a voice said, 'Mr Quail is under sedation now, sir. Do you want to supervise this one, or shall we go ahead?'

'It's routine,' McClane observed. 'You may go ahead, Lowe; I don't think you'll run into any trouble.' Programming an artificial memory of a trip to another planet – with or without the added **fillip** of being a secret agent – showed up on the firm's work schedule with monotonous regularity. *In one month*, he calculated **wryly**, *we must do twenty of these . . .* **ersatz** *interplanetary travel has become our bread and butter*.

'Whatever you say, Mr McClane,' Lowe's voice came, and thereupon the intercom shut off.

Going to the vault section in the chamber behind his office, McClane searched about for a Three packet – trip to Mars – and a Sixty-two packet; secret Interplan spy.

---

fillip: a kick, a stimulation
wryly: with a twisted sense of humour
ersatz: fake

Finding the two packets, he returned with them to his desk, seated himself comfortably, poured out the contents – merchandise which would be planted in Quail's conapt while the lab technicians busied themselves installing the false memory.

A one-poscred sneaky-pete side arm, McClane reflected; *that's the largest item. Sets us back financially the most.* Then a pellet-sized transmitter, which could be swallowed if the agent were caught. Code book that astonishingly resembled the real thing . . . the firm's models were highly accurate: based, whenever possible, on actual US military issue. Odd bits which made no intrinsic sense but which would be woven into the warp and woof of Quail's imaginary trip, would coincide with his memory: half an ancient silver 50-cent piece, several quotations from John Donne's sermons written incorrectly, each on a separate piece of transparent tissue-thin paper, several match folders from bars on Mars, a stainless steel spoon engraved PROPERTY OF DOME–MARS NATIONAL KIBBUZIM, a wire tapping coil which –

The intercom buzzed. 'Mr McClane, I'm sorry to bother you but something rather ominous has come up. Maybe it would be better if you were in here after all. Quail is already under sedation; he reacted well to the narkidrine; he's completely unconscious and receptive. But –'

'I'll be in.' Sensing trouble, McClane left his office; a moment later he emerged in the work area.

On a hygienic bed lay Douglas Quail, breathing slowly and regularly, his eyes virtually shut; he seemed dimly – but only dimly – aware of the two technicians and now McClane himself.

'There's no space to insert false memory-patterns?' McClane felt irritation. 'Merely drop out two work weeks; he's employed as a clerk at the West Coast Emigration Bureau, which is a government agency, so he undoubtedly has or had two weeks vacation within the last year. That ought to do it.' Petty details annoyed him. And always would.

'Our problem,' Lowe said sharply, 'is something quite different.' He bent over the bed, said to Quail, 'Tell Mr McClane what you told us.' To McClane he said, 'Listen closely.'

The grey-green eyes of the man lying **supine** in the bed focused on McClane's face. The eyes, he observed uneasily, had become hard; they had a polished, inorganic quality, like semi-precious tumbled stones. He was not sure that he liked what he saw; the brilliance was too cold. 'What do you want now?' Quail said harshly. 'You've broken my cover. Get out of here before I take you all apart.' He studied McClane. 'Especially you,' he continued. 'You're in charge of this counter-operation.'

Lowe said, 'How long were you on Mars?'

'One month,' Quail said gratingly.

'And your purpose there?' Lowe demanded.

The meagre lips twisted; Quail eyed him and did not speak. At last, drawling the words out so that they dripped with hostility, he said, 'Agent for Interplan. As I already told you. Don't you record everything that's said? Play your vid-aud tape back for your boss and leave me alone.' He shut his eyes, then; the hard brilliance ceased. McClane felt, instantly, a rushing splurge of relief.

Lowe said quietly, 'This is a tough man, Mr McClane.'

'He won't be,' McClane said, 'after we arrange for him to lose his memory-chain again. He'll be as meek as before.' To Quail he said, 'So *this* is why you wanted to go to Mars so terribly badly.'

Without opening his eyes Quail said, 'I never wanted to go to Mars. I was assigned it – they handed it to me and there I was: stuck. Oh yeah, I admit I was curious about

---

supine: on his back

it; who wouldn't be?' Again he opened his eyes and surveyed the three of them, McClane in particular. 'Quite a truth drug you've got here; it brought up things I had absolutely no memory of.' He pondered. 'I wonder about Kirsten,' he said, half to himself. 'Could she be in on it? An Interplan contact keeping an eye on me . . . to be certain I didn't regain my memory? No wonder she's been so derisive about my wanting to go there.' Faintly, he smiled; the smile – one of understanding – disappeared almost at once.

McClane said, 'Please believe me, Mr Quail; we stumbled onto this entirely by accident. In the work we do –'

'I believe you,' Quail said. He seemed tired, now; the drug was continuing to pull him under, deeper and deeper. 'Where did I say I'd been?' he murmured. 'Mars? Hard to remember – I know I'd like to see it; so would everybody else. But me –' His voice trailed off. 'Just a clerk, a nothing clerk.'

Straightening up, Lowe said to his superior, 'He wants a false memory implanted that corresponds to a trip he actually took. And a false reason which is the real reason. He's telling the truth; he's a long way down in the narkidrine. The trip is very vivid in his mind – at least under sedation. But apparently he doesn't recall it otherwise. Someone, probably at a government military-sciences lab, erased his conscious memories; all he knew was that going to Mars meant something special to him, and so did being a secret agent. They couldn't erase that; it's not a memory but a desire, undoubtedly the same one that motivated him to volunteer for the assignment in the first place.'

The other technician, Keeler, said to McClane, 'What do we do? Graft a false memory-pattern over the real memory? There's no telling what the results would be; he might remember some of the genuine trip, and the confusion might bring on a psychotic interlude. He'd have to hold two opposite premises in his mind simultaneously: that he went to Mars and that he didn't. That he's a genuine agent for Interplan and he's not, that it's spurious. I think we ought to revive him without any false memory implantation and send him out of here; this is hot.'

'Agreed,' McClane said. A thought came to him. 'Can you predict what he'll remember when he comes out of sedation?'

'Impossible to tell,' Lowe said. 'He probably will have some dim, diffuse memory of his actual trip, now. And he'd probably be in grave doubt as to its validity; he'd probably decide our programming slipped a gear-tooth. And he'd remember coming here; that wouldn't be erased – unless you want it erased.'

'The less we mess with this man,' McClane said, 'the better I like it. This is nothing for us to fool around with; we've been foolish enough to – or unlucky enough to – uncover a genuine Interplan spy who has a cover so perfect that up to now even he didn't know what he was – or rather is.' The sooner they washed their hands of the man calling himself Douglas Quail the better.

'Are you going to plant packets Three and Sixty-two in his conapt?' Lowe said.

'No,' McClane said. 'And we're going to return half his fee.'

'"Half!" Why half?'

McClane said lamely, 'It seems to be a good compromise.'

As the cab carried him back to his conapt at the residential end of Chicago, Douglas Quail said to himself, *It's sure good to be back on Terra.*

Already the month-long period on Mars had begun to waver in his memory; he had only an image of profound gaping craters, an ever-present ancient erosion of hills, of vitality, of motion itself. A world of dust where little happened, where a good part of the day was spent checking and rechecking one's portable oxygen source. And then the life forms, the unassuming and modest grey-brown cacti and maw-worms.

As a matter of fact he had brought back several moribund examples of Martian fauna; he had smuggled them through customs. After all, they posed no menace; they couldn't survive in Earth's heavy atmosphere.

Reaching into his coat pocket, he rummaged for the container of Martian maw-worms –

And found an envelope instead.

Lifting it out, he discovered, to his perplexity, that it contained 570 poscreds, in cred bills of low denomination.

Where'd I get this? he asked himself. *Didn't I spend every 'cred I had on my trip?*

With the money came a slip of paper marked: *One-half fee ret'd. By McClane.* And then the date. Today's date.

'Recall,' he said aloud.

'Recall what, sir or madam?' the robot driver of the cab inquired respectfully.

'Do you have a phone book?' Quail demanded.

'Certainly, sir or madam.' A slot opened; from it slid a microtape phone book for Cook County.

'It's spelled oddly,' Quail said as he leafed through the pages of the yellow section. He felt fear, then; abiding fear. 'Here it is,' he said. 'Take me there, to Rekal, Incorporated. I've changed my mind; I don't want to go home.'

'Yes sir, or madam, as the case may be,' the driver said. A moment later the cab was zipping back in the opposite direction.

'May I make use of your phone?' he asked.

'Be my guest,' the robot driver said. And presented a shiny new emperor 3-D colour phone to him.

He dialled his own conapt. And after a pause found himself confronted by a miniature but chillingly realistic image of Kirsten on the small screen. 'I've been to Mars,' he said to her.

'You're drunk.' Her lips writhed scornfully. 'Or worse.'

''S god's truth.'

'When?' she demanded.

'I don't know.' He felt confused. 'A simulated trip, I think. By means of one of those artificial or extra-factual or whatever it is memory places. It didn't take.'

Kirsten said witheringly, 'You *are* drunk.' And broke the connection at her end. He hung up, then, feeling his face flush. *Always the same tone*, he said hotly to himself. *Always the retort, as if she knows everything and I know nothing. What a marriage. Keerist*, he thought dismally.

A moment later the cab stopped at the curb before a modern, very attractive little pink building, over which a shifting, polychromatic neon sign read: REKAL, INCORPORATED.

The receptionist, chic and bare from the waist up, started in surprise, then gained masterful control of herself. 'Oh, hello, Mr Quail,' she said nervously. 'H-how are you? Did you forget something?'

'The rest of my fee back,' he said.

More composed now the receptionist said, 'Fee? I think you are mistaken, Mr Quail. You were here discussing the feasibility of an extra-factual trip for you, but –' She shrugged her smooth pale shoulders. 'As I understand it, no trip was taken.'

Quail said, 'I remember everything, miss. My letter to Rekal, Incorporated, which started this whole business off. I remember my arrival here, my visit with Mr McClane. Then the two lab technicians taking me in tow and administering a drug to put me out.' No wonder the firm had returned half his fee. The false memory of his 'trip to

Mars' hadn't taken – at least not entirely, not as he had been assured.

'Mr Quail,' the girl said, 'although you are a minor clerk you are a good-looking man and it spoils your features to become angry. If it would make you feel any better, I might, ahem, let you take me out . . .'

He felt furious, then. 'I remember you,' he said savagely. 'For instance the fact that your breasts are sprayed blue; that stuck in my mind. And I remember Mr McClane's promise that if I remembered my visit to Rekal, Incorporated I'd receive my money back in full. Where is Mr McClane?'

After a delay – probably as long as they could manage – he found himself once more seated facing the imposing walnut desk, exactly as he had been an hour or so earlier in the day.

'Some technique you have,' Quail said sardonically. His disappointment – and resentment – was enormous, by now. 'My so-called "memory" of a trip to Mars as an undercover agent for Interplan is hazy and vague and shot full of contradictions. And I clearly remember my dealings here with you people. I ought to take this to the Better Business Bureau.' He was burning angry, at this point; his sense of being cheated had overwhelmed him, had destroyed his customary aversion to participating in a public squabble.

Looking morose, as well as cautious, McClane said, 'We capitulate, Quail. We'll refund the balance of your fee. I fully concede the fact that we did absolutely nothing for you.' His tone was resigned.

Quail said accusingly, 'You didn't even provide me with the various artefacts that you claimed would "prove" to me I had been on Mars. All that song-and-dance you went into – it hasn't materialised into a damn thing. Not even a ticket stub. Nor postcards. Nor passport. Nor proof of immunisation shots. Nor –'

'Listen, Quail,' McClane said. 'Suppose I told you
–' He broke off. 'Let it go.' He pressed a button on his
intercom. 'Shirley, will you disburse 570 more 'creds
in the form of a cashier's cheque made out to Douglas
Quail? Thank you.' He released the button, then glared
at Quail.

Presently the cheque appeared; the receptionist placed
it before McClane and once more vanished out of sight,
leaving the two men alone, still facing each other across
the surface of the massive walnut desk.

'Let me give you a word of advice,' McClane said as he
signed the cheque and passed it over, 'Don't discuss your,
ahem, recent trip to Mars with anyone.'

'What trip?'

'Well, that's the thing.' Doggedly, McClane said, 'The
trip you partially remember. Act as if you don't
remember; pretend it never took place. Don't ask me
why; just take my advice: it'll be better for all of us.' He
had begun to perspire. Freely. 'Now, Mr Quail, I have
other business, other clients to see.' He rose, showed
Quail to the door.

Quail said, as he opened the door, 'A firm that turns out
such bad work shouldn't have any clients at all.' He shut
the door behind him.

On the way home in the cab Quail pondered the
wording of his letter of complaint to the Better Business
Bureau, Terra Division. As soon as he could get to his
typewriter he'd get started; it was clearly his duty to warn
other people away from Rekal, Incorporated.

When he got back to his conapt he seated himself
before his Hermes Rocket portable, opened the drawers
and rummaged for carbon paper – and noticed a small,
familiar box. A box which he had carefully filled on Mars
with Martian fauna and later smuggled through customs.

Opening the box he saw, to his disbelief, six dead maw-
worms and several varieties of the unicellular life on

which the Martian worms fed. The **protozoa** were dried-up, dusty, but he recognised them; it had taken him an entire day picking among the vast dark alien boulders to find them. A wonderful, illuminated journey of discovery.

But I didn't go to Mars, he realised.

Yet on the other hand –

Kirsten appeared at the doorway to the room, an armload of pale-brown groceries gripped. 'Why are you home in the middle of the day?' Her voice, in an eternity of sameness, was accusing.

'*Did I go to Mars?*' he asked her. 'You would know.'

'No, of course you didn't go to Mars; *you* would know that. I would think. Aren't you always bleating about going?'

He said, 'By God, I think I went.' After a pause he added, 'And simultaneously I think I didn't go.'

'Make up your mind.'

'How can I?' He gestured. 'I have both memory-tracks grafted inside my head; one is real and one isn't but I can't tell which is which. Why can't I rely on you? They haven't tinkered with you.' She could do this much for him at least – even if she never did anything else.

Kirsten said in a level, controlled voice, 'Doug, if you don't pull yourself together, we're through. I'm going to leave you.'

'I'm in trouble.' His voice came out husky and coarse. And shaking. 'Probably I'm heading into a psychotic episode; I hope not, but – maybe that's it. It would explain everything, anyhow.'

Setting down the bag of groceries, Kirsten stalked to the closet. 'I was not kidding,' she said to him quietly. She brought out a coat, got it on, walked back to the door of the conapt. 'I'll phone you one of these days soon,' she said tonelessly. 'This is goodbye, Doug. I hope you pull out of this eventually; I really pray you do. For your sake.'

---

protozoa: one-celled animals

'Wait,' he said desperately. 'Just tell me and make it absolute; I did go or I didn't – tell me which one.' *But they may have altered your memory-track also*, he realised.

The door closed. His wife had left. Finally!

A voice behind him said, 'Well, that's that. Now put up your hands, Quail. And also please turn around and face this way.'

He turned, instinctively, without raising his hands.

The man who faced him wore the plum uniform of the Interplan Police Agency, and his gun appeared to be UN issue. And, for some odd reason, he seemed familiar to Quail; familiar in a blurred, distorted fashion which he could not pin down. So, jerkily, he raised his hands.

'You remember,' the policeman said, 'your trip to Mars. We know all your actions today and all your thoughts – in particular your very important thoughts on the trip home from Rekal, Incorporated.' He explained, 'We have a telep-transmitter wired within your skull; it keeps us constantly informed.'

A telepathic transmitter; use of a living **plasma** that had been discovered on Luna. He shuddered with self-aversion. The thing lived inside him, within his own brain, feeding, listening, feeding. But the Interplan police used them; that had come out even in the homeopapes. So this was probably true, dismal as it was.

'Why me?' Quail said huskily. What had he done – or thought? And what did this have to do with Rekal, Incorporated?

'Fundamentally,' the Interplan cop said, 'this has nothing to do with Rekal; it's between you and us.' He tapped his right ear. 'I'm still picking up your mentational processes by way of your **cephalic** transmitter.' In the

---

plasma: the colourless part of blood or milk
cephalic: belonging to the head

man's ear Quail saw a small white-plastic plug. 'So I have to warn you: anything you think may be held against you.' He smiled. 'Not that it matters now; you've already thought and spoken yourself into oblivion. What's annoying is the fact that under narkidrine at Rekal, Incorporated you told them, their technicians and the owner, Mr McClane, about your trip – where you went, for whom, some of what you did. They're very frightened. They wish they had never laid eyes on you.' He added reflectively, 'They're right.'

Quail said, 'I never made any trip. It's a false memory-chain improperly planted in me by McClane's technicians.' But then he thought of the box, in his desk drawer, containing the Martian life forms. And the trouble and hardship he had had gathering them. The memory seemed real. And the box of life forms; that certainly was real. Unless McClane had planted it. Perhaps this was one of the 'proofs' which McClane had talked glibly about.

The memory of my trip to Mars, he thought, *doesn't convince me – but unfortunately it has convinced the Interplan Police Agency. They think I really went to Mars and they think I at least partially realise it.*

'We not only know you went to Mars,' the Interplan cop agreed, in answer to his thoughts, 'but we know that you now remember enough to be difficult for us. And there's no use **expunging** your conscious memory of all this, because if we do you'll simply show up at Rekal, Incorporated again and start over. And we can't do anything about McClane and his operation because we have no **jurisdiction** over anyone except our own people. Anyhow, McClane hasn't committed any crime.' He eyed Quail. 'Nor, technically, have you. You didn't go to Rekal, Incorporated with the idea of regaining your memory;

---

expunging: erasing
jurisdiction: legal authority

you went, as we realise, for the usual reason people go there – a love by plain, dull people for adventure.' He added, 'Unfortunately you're not plain, not dull, and you've already had too much excitement; the last thing in the universe you needed was a course from Rekal, Incorporated. Nothing could have been more lethal for you or for us. And, for that matter, for McClane.'

Quail said, 'Why is it "difficult" for you if I remember my trip – my alleged trip – and what I did there?'

'Because,' the Interplan harness bull said, 'what you did is not in accord with our great white all-protecting father public image. You did, for us, what we never do. As you'll presently remember – thanks to narkidrine. That box of dead worms and algae has been sitting in your desk drawer for six months, ever since you got back. And at no time have you shown the slightest curiosity about it. We didn't even know you had it until you remembered it on your way home from Rekal; then we came here on the double to look for it.' He added, unnecessarily, 'Without any luck; there wasn't enough time.'

A second Interplan cop joined the first one; the two briefly conferred. Meanwhile, Quail thought rapidly. He did remember more, now; the cop had been right about narkidrine. They – Interplan – probably used it themselves. Probably? He knew darn well they did; he had seen them putting a prisoner on it. Where would *that* be? Somewhere on Terra? More likely Luna, he decided, viewing the image rising from his highly defective – but rapidly less so – memory.

And he remembered something else. Their reason for sending him to Mars; the job he had done.

No wonder they had expunged his memory.

'Oh god,' the first of the two Interplan cops said, breaking off his conversation with his companion. Obviously, he had picked up Quail's thoughts. 'Well, this is a far worse problem, now; as bad as it can get.' He walked towards Quail, again covering him with his gun. 'We've got to kill you,' he said. 'And right away.'

Nervously, his fellow officer said, 'Why right away? Can't we simply cart him off to Interplan New York and let them –'

'*He* knows why it has to be right away,' the first cop said; he too looked nervous, now, but Quail realised that it was for an entirely different reason. His memory had been brought back almost entirely, now. And he fully understood the officer's tension.

'On Mars,' Quail said hoarsely, 'I killed a man. After getting past fifteen bodyguards. Some armed with sneaky-pete guns, the way you are.' He had been trained, by Interplan, over a five-year period to be an assassin. A professional killer. He knew ways to take out armed adversaries . . . such as these two officers; and the one with the ear-receiver knew it, too.

If he moved swiftly enough –

The gun fired. But he had already moved to one side, and at the same time he chopped down the gun-carrying officer. In an instant he had possession of the gun and was covering the other, confused, officer.

'Picked my thoughts up,' Quail said, panting for breath. 'He knew what I was going to do, but I did it anyhow.'

Half sitting up, the injured officer grated, 'He won't use that gun on you, Sam; I pick that up, too. He knows he's finished, and he knows we know it, too. Come on, Quail.' Laboriously, grunting with pain, he got shakily to his feet. He held out his hand. 'The gun,' he said to Quail. 'You can't use it, and if you turn it over to me I'll guarantee not to kill you; you'll be given a hearing, and someone higher up in Interplan will decide, not me. Maybe they can erase your memory once more; I don't know. But you know the thing I was going to kill you for; I couldn't keep you from remembering it. So my reason for wanting to kill you is in a sense past.'

Quail, clutching the gun, bolted from the conapt, sprinted for the elevator. *If you follow me*, he thought. *I'll kill you. So don't*. He jabbed at the elevator button and, a moment later, the doors slid back.

The police hadn't followed him. Obviously they had picked up his terse, tense thoughts and had decided not to take the chance.

With him inside the elevator descended. He had gotten away – for a time. But what next? Where could he go?

The elevator reached the ground floor; a moment later Quail had joined the mob of peds hurrying along the runnels. His head ached and he felt sick. But at least he had evaded death; they had come very close to shooting him on the spot, back in his own conapt.

And they probably will again, he decided. *When they find me. And with this transmitter inside me, that won't take too long.*

Ironically, he had gotten exactly what he had asked Rekal, Incorporated for. Adventure, peril, Interplan police at work, a secret and dangerous trip to Mars in which his life was at stake – everything he had wanted as a false memory.

The advantages of it being a memory – and nothing more – could now be appreciated.

On a park bench, alone, he sat dully watching a flock of perts; a semi-bird imported from Mars' two moons, capable of soaring flight even against Earth's huge gravity.

Maybe I can find my way back to Mars, he pondered. But then what? It would be worse on Mars; the political organisation whose leader he had assassinated would spot him the moment he stepped from the ship; he would have Interplan and *them* after him, there.

Can you hear me thinking? he wondered. Easy avenue to paranoia; sitting here alone he felt them tuning in on him, monitoring, recording, discussing . . . He shivered, rose to his feet, walked aimlessly, his hands deep in his pockets. *No matter where I go*, he realised, *you'll always be with me. As long as I have this device inside my head.*

I'll make a deal with you, he thought to himself – and to them. *Can't you imprint a false-memory template on me again, as you did before, that I lived an average, routine life, never went to Mars? Never saw an Interplan uniform up close and never handled a gun?*

A voice inside his brain answered, 'As has been carefully explained to you: that would not be enough.'

Astonished, he halted.

'We formerly communicated with you in this manner,' the voice continued. 'When you were operating in the field, on Mars. It's been months since we've done it; we assumed in fact, that we'd never have to do so again. Where are you?'

'Walking,' Quail said, 'to my death.' *By your officers' guns*, he added as an afterthought. 'How can you be sure it wouldn't be enough?' he demanded. 'Don't the Rekal techniques work?'

'As we said. If you're given a set of standard, average memories you get – restless. You'd inevitably seek out Rekal or one of its competitors again. We can't go through this a second time.'

'Suppose,' Quail said, 'once my authentic memories have been cancelled, something more vital than standard memories are implanted. Something which would act to satisfy my craving,' he said. 'That's been proved; that's probably why you initially hired me. But you ought to be able to come up with something else – something equal. I was the richest man on Terra but I finally gave all my money to educational foundations. Or I was a famous deep-space explorer. Anything of that sort; wouldn't one of those do?'

Silence.

'Try it,' he said desperately. 'Get some of your top-notch military psychiatrists; explore my mind. Find out what my most expansive daydream is.' He tried to think. 'Women,' he said. 'Thousands of them, like Don Juan had. An interplanetary playboy – a mistress in every city on Earth, Luna and Mars. Only I gave that up, out of exhaustion. Please,' he begged. 'Try it.'

'You'd voluntarily surrender, then?' the voice inside his head asked. 'If we agreed, to arrange such a solution? *If it's possible?*'

After an interval of hesitation he said, 'Yes.' *I'll take the risk*, he said to himself, *that you don't simply kill me*.

'You make the first move,' the voice said presently. 'Turn yourself over to us. And we'll investigate that line of possibility. If we can't do it, however, if your authentic memories begin to crop up again as they've done at this time, then –' There was silence and then the voice finished, 'We'll have to destroy you. As you must understand. Well, Quail, you still want to try?'

'Yes,' he said. Because the alternative was death now – and for certain. At least this way he had a chance, slim as it was.

'You present yourself at our main barracks in New York,' the voice of the Interplan cop resumed. 'At 580 Fifth Avenue, floor twelve. Once you've surrendered yourself we'll have our psychiatrists begin on you; we'll have personality-profile tests made. We'll attempt to determine your absolute, ultimate fantasy wish – then we'll bring you back to Rekal, Incorporated, here; get them in on it, fulfilling that wish in **vicarious surrogate retrospection**. And – good luck. We do owe you something; you acted as a capable instrument for us.' The voice lacked malice; if anything, they – the organisation – felt sympathy towards him.

---

vicarious surrogate retrospection: a memory that will seem real, even though it never happened

'Thanks,' Quail said. And began searching for a robot cab.

'Mr Quail,' the stern-faced, elderly Interplan psychiatrist said, 'you possess a most interesting wish-fulfilment dream fantasy. Probably nothing such as you consciously entertain or suppose. This is commonly the way; I hope it won't upset you too much to hear about it.'

The senior ranking Interplan officer present said briskly, 'He better not be too much upset to hear about it, not if he expects not to get shot.'

'Unlike the fantasy of wanting to be an Interplan undercover agent,' the psychiatrist continued, 'which, being relatively speaking a product of maturity, had a certain plausibility to it, this production is a grotesque dream of your childhood; it is no wonder you fail to recall it. Your fantasy is this; you are nine years old, walking alone down a rustic lane. An unfamiliar variety of space vessel from another star-system lands directly in front of you. No one on Earth but you, Mr Quail, sees it. The creatures within are very small and helpless, somewhat on the order of field mice, although they are attempting to invade Earth; tens of thousands of other such ships will soon be on their way, when this advance party gives the go-ahead signal.'

'And I suppose I stop them,' Quail said, experiencing a mixture of amusement and disgust. 'Single-handed I wipe them out. Probably by stepping on them with my foot.'

'No,' the psychiatrist said patiently. 'You halt the invasion, but not by destroying them. Instead, you show them kindness and mercy even though by telepathy – their mode of communication – you know why they have come. They have never seen such humane traits exhibited by any sentient organism, and to show their appreciation they make a covenant with you.'

Quail said, 'They won't invade Earth as long as I'm alive.'

'Exactly.' To the Interplan officer the psychiatrist said, 'You can see it does fit his personality, despite his feigned scorn.'

'So by merely existing,' Quail said, feeling a growing pleasure, 'by simply being alive, I keep Earth safe from alien rule. I'm in effect, then, the most important person on Terra. Without lifting a finger.'

'Yes indeed, sir,' the psychiatrist said. 'And this is bedrock in your psyche; this is a life-long childhood fantasy. Which, without depth and drug therapy, you never would have recalled. But it has always existed in you; it went underneath, but never ceased.'

To McClane, who sat intently listening, the senior police official said, 'Can you implant an extra-factual memory pattern that extreme in him?'

'We get handed every possible type of wish-fantasy there is,' McClane said. 'Frankly, I've heard a lot worse than this. Certainly we can handle it. Twenty-four hours from now he won't just *wish* he'd saved Earth; he'll devoutly believe it really happened.'

The senior police official said, 'You can start the job, then. In preparation we've already once again erased the memory in him of his trip to Mars.'

Quail said, 'What trip to Mars?'

No one answered him, so, reluctantly, he shelved the question. And anyhow a police vehicle had now put in its appearance; he, McClane and the senior police officer crowded into it, and presently they were on their way to Chicago and Rekal, Incorporated.

'You had better make no errors this time,' the police officer said to heavy-set, nervous-looking McClane.

'I can't see what could go wrong,' McClane mumbled, perspiring. 'This has nothing to do with Mars or Interplan. Single-handedly stopping an invasion of Earth from another star-system.' He shook his head at that. 'Wow, what a kid dreams up. And by pious virtue, too; not by force. It's sort of quaint.' He dabbed at his forehead with a large linen pocket handkerchief.

Nobody said anything.

'In fact,' McClane said, 'it's touching.'

'But arrogant,' the police official said starkly. 'Inasmuch as when he dies the invasion will resume. No wonder he doesn't recall it; it's the most grandiose fantasy I ever ran across.' He eyed Quail with disapproval. 'And to think we put this man on our payroll.'

When they reached Rekal, Incorporated the receptionist, Shirley, met them breathlessly in the outer office. 'Welcome back, Mr Quail,' she fluttered, her melon-shaped breasts – today painted an incandescent orange – bobbing with agitation. 'I'm sorry everything worked out so badly before; I'm sure this time it'll go better.'

Still repeatedly dabbing at his shiny forehead with his neatly-folded Irish linen handkerchief, McClane said, 'It better.' Moving with rapidity he rounded up Lowe and Keeler, escorted them and Douglas Quail to the work area, and then, with Shirley and the senior police officer, returned to his familiar office. To wait.

'Do we have a packet made up for this, Mr McClane?' Shirley asked, bumping against him in her agitation, then colouring modestly.

'I think we do.' He tried to recall, then gave up and consulted the formal chart. 'A combination,' he decided aloud, 'of packets Eighty-one, Twenty, and Six.' From the vault section of the chamber behind his desk he fished out the appropriate packets, carried them to his desk for inspection. 'From Eighty-one,' he explained, 'a magic healing rod given him – the client in question, this time Mr Quail – by the race of beings from another system. A token of their gratitude.'

'Does it work?' the police officer asked curiously.

'It did once,' McClane explained. 'But he, ahem, you see, used it up years ago, healing right and left. Now it's only a memento. But he remembers it working spectacularly.' He chuckled, then opened packet Twenty. 'Document from the UN Secretary General thanking him for saving Earth; this isn't precisely appropriate, because part of Quail's fantasy is that no one knows of the invasion except himself, but for the sake of verisimilitude we'll throw it in.' He inspected packet Six, then. What came from this? He couldn't recall; frowning, he dug into the plastic bag as Shirley and the Interplan police officer watched intently.

'Writing,' Shirley said. 'In a funny language.'

'This tells who they were,' McClane said, 'and where they came from. Including a detailed star map logging their flight here and the system of origin. Of course it's in *their* script, so he can't read it. But he remembers them reading it to him in his own tongue.' He placed the three artefacts in the centre of the desk. 'These should be taken to Quail's conapt,' he said to the police officer. 'So that when he gets home he'll find them. And it'll confirm his fantasy. SOP – standard operating procedure.' He chuckled apprehensively, wondering how matters were going with Lowe and Keeler.

The intercom buzzed. 'Mr McClane, I'm sorry to bother you.' It was Lowe's voice; he froze as he recognised it, froze and became mute. 'But something's come up. Maybe it would be better if you came in here and supervised. Like before, Quail reacted well to the narkidrine; he's unconscious, relaxed and receptive. But –'

McClane sprinted for the work area.

On a hygienic bed Douglas Quail lay breathing slowly and regularly, eyes half-shut, dimly conscious of those round him.

'We started interrogating him,' Lowe said, white-faced. 'To find out exactly when to place the fantasy-memory of him single-handedly having saved Earth. And strangely enough –'

'They told me not to tell,' Douglas Quail mumbled in a dull drug-saturated voice. 'That was the agreement. I wasn't even supposed to remember. But how could I forget an event like that?'

I guess it would be hard, McClane reflected. *But you did – until now.*

'They even gave me a scroll,' Quail mumbled, 'of gratitude. I have it hidden in my conapt; I'll show it to you.'

To the Interplan officer who had followed after him, McClane said, 'Well, I offer the suggestion that you better not kill him. If you do they'll return.'

'They also gave me a magic invisible destroying rod,' Quail mumbled, eyes totally shut, now. 'That's how I killed that man on Mars you sent me to take out. It's in my drawer along with the box of Martian maw-worms and dried-up plant life.'

Wordlessly, the Interplan officer turned and stalked from the work area.

I might as well put those packets of proof-artefacts away, McClane said to himself resignedly. He walked, step by step, back to his office. *Including the citation from the UN Secretary General. After all –*

The real one probably would not be long in coming.

The Eyes Have It
Philip K. Dick

Philip K. Dick again, but this time in playful mood. Spoofs of alien invasion (and writers' love of similes and metaphors) don't come much whackier than this.

It was quite by accident I discovered this incredible invasion of Earth by life forms from another planet. As yet, I haven't done anything about it; I can't think of anything to do. I wrote to the government, and they sent back a pamphlet on the repair and maintenance of frame houses. Anyhow, the whole thing is known; I'm not the first to discover it. Maybe it's even under control.

I was sitting in my easy chair, idly turning the pages of a paperback book someone had left on the bus, when I came across the reference that first put me on the trail. For a moment I didn't respond. It took some time for the full import to sink in. After I'd comprehended, it seemed odd I hadn't noticed it right away.

The reference was clearly to a non-human species of incredible properties, not **indigenous** to Earth. A species, I hasten to point out, customarily **masquerading** as ordinary human beings. Their disguise, however, became transparent in the face of the following observations by the author. It was at once obvious the author knew everything. Knew everything – and was taking it in his stride. The line (and I tremble remembering it even now) read:

> . . . *his eyes slowly roved about the room.*

indigenous: belonging naturally to an area
masquerading: pretending

Vague chills assailed me. I tried to picture the eyes. Did they roll like **dimes**? The passage indicated not; they seemed to move through the air, not over the surface. Rather rapidly, apparently. No one in the story was surprised. That's what tipped me off. No sign of amazement at such an outrageous thing. Later the matter was amplified.

> . . . *his eyes moved from person to person.*

There it was in a nutshell. The eyes had clearly come apart from the rest of him and were on their own. My heart pounded and my breath choked in my windpipe. I had stumbled on an accidental mention of a totally unfamiliar race. Obviously non-Terrestrial. Yet, to the characters in the book, it was perfectly natural – which suggested they belonged to the same species.

And the author? A slow suspicion burned in my mind. The author was taking it rather *too easily* in his stride. Evidently, he felt this was quite a usual thing. He made absolutely no attempt to conceal this knowledge. The story continued:

> . . . *presently his eyes fastened on Julia.*

Julia, being a lady, had at least the breeding to feel indignant. She is described as blushing and knitting her brows angrily. At this, I sighed with relief. They weren't *all* non-Terrestrials. The narrative continues:

> . . . *slowly, calmly, his eyes examined every inch of her.*

Great Scott! But here the girl turned and stomped off and the matter ended. I lay back in my chair gasping with horror. My wife and family regarded me in wonder.

'What's wrong, dear?' my wife asked.

---

dime: a US coin (one tenth of a dollar)

I couldn't tell her. Knowledge like this was too much for the ordinary run-of-the-mill person. I had to keep it to myself. 'Nothing,' I gasped. I leaped up, snatched the book, and hurried out of the room.

In the garage, I continued reading. There was more. Trembling, I read the next revealing passage:

> . . . *he put his arm around Julia. Presently she asked him if he would remove his arm. He immediately did so, with a smile.*

It's not said what was done with the arm after the fellow had removed it. Maybe it was left standing upright in the corner. Maybe it was thrown away. I don't care. In any case, the full meaning was there, staring me right in the face.

Here was a race of creatures capable of removing portions of their anatomy at will. Eyes, arms – and maybe more. Without batting an eyelash. My knowledge of biology came in handy, at this point. Obviously they were simple beings, uni-cellular, some sort of primitive single-celled things. Beings no more developed than starfish. Starfish can do the same thing, you know.

I read on. And came to this incredible revelation, tossed off cooly by the author without the faintest tremour:

> . . . *outside the movie theater we split up. Part of us went inside, part over to the cafe for dinner.*

Binary fission, obviously. Splitting in half and forming two entities. Probably each lower half went to the café, it being farther, and the upper halves to the movies. I read on, hands shaking. I had really stumbled onto something here. My mind reeled as I made out this passage:

> . . . *I'm afraid there's no doubt about it. Poor Bibney has lost his head again.*

Which was followed by:

. . . and Bob says he has utterly no guts.

Yet Bibney got around as well as the next person. The next person, however, was just as strange. He was soon described as:

. . . totally lacking in brains.

There was no doubt of the thing in the next passage. Julia, whom I had thought to be the one normal person, reveals herself as also being an alien life form, similar to the rest:

. . . quite deliberately, Julia had given her heart to the young man.

It didn't relate what the final disposition of the organ was, but I didn't really care. It was evident Julia had gone right on living in her usual manner, like all the others in the book. Without heart, arms, eyes, brains, viscera, dividing up in two when the occasion demanded. Without a **qualm**.

. . . thereupon she gave him her hand.

I sickened. The rascal now had her hand, as well as her heart. I shudder to think what he's done with them, by this time.

. . . he took her arm.

Not content to wait, he had to start dismantling her on his own. Flushing crimson, I slammed the book shut and leaped to my feet. But not in time to escape one last reference to those carefree bits of anatomy whose travels had originally thrown me on the track:

. . . her eyes followed him all the way down the road and across the meadow.

---

qualm: a misgiving

I rushed from the garage and back inside the warm house, as if the accursed things were following *me*. My wife and children were playing Monopoly in the kitchen. I joined them and played with frantic fervour, brow feverish, teeth chattering.

I had had enough of the thing. I want to hear no more about it. Let them come on. Let them invade Earth. I don't want to get mixed up in it.

I have absolutely no stomach for it.

The Laxian Key

Robert Sheckley

Stories about the misadventures of space-hopping double acts were popular in magazine fiction. Several of Isaac Asimov's robot stories feature the hapless Powell and Donovan, and John W. Campbell, the editor of *Astounding Science Fiction*, wrote a number of tales featuring Penton and Blake.

Robert Sheckley's novels (such as *Mindswap*, *Options* and *Dimension of Miracles*) and stories (in collections such as *The Robot Who Looked Like Me*) burst with zany situations and bizarre ideas. Years before the movie *Space Cowboys*, ill-starred space-jocks Arnold and Gregor were spreading their own unique brand of chaos through the galaxy . . .

Richard Gregor was at his desk in the dusty office of the AAA Ace Interplanetary Decontamination Service. It was almost noon, but Arnold, his partner, hadn't showed up yet. Gregor was just laying out an unusually complicated game of **solitaire**. Then he heard a loud crash in the hall.

The door of AAA Ace opened, and Arnold stuck his head in.

'Banker's hours?' Gregor asked.

'I have just made our fortunes,' Arnold said. He threw the door fully open and beckoned dramatically. 'Bring it in, boys.'

Four sweating workmen lugged in a square black machine the size of a baby elephant.

---

solitaire: a game played by one person

'There it is,' Arnold said proudly. He paid the workmen, and stood, hands clasped behind his back, eyes half-shut, surveying the machine.

Gregor put his cards away with the slow, weary motions of a man who has seen everything. He stood up and walked around the machine. 'All right, I give up. What is it?'

'It's a million bucks, right in our fists.' Arnold said.

'Of course. But *what* is it?'

'It's a Free Producer,' Arnold said. He smiled proudly. 'I was walking past Joe's Interstellar Junkyard this morning, and there it was, sitting in the window. I picked it up for next to nothing. Joe didn't even know what it was.'

'I don't either,' Gregor said. 'Do you?'

Arnold was on his hands and knees, trying to read the instructions engraved on the front of the machine. Without looking up, he said, 'You've heard of the planet Meldge, haven't you?'

Gregor nodded. Meldge was a third-rate little planet on the northern **periphery** of the galaxy, some distance from the trade routes. At one time, Meldge had possessed an extremely advanced civilisation, made possible by the so-called Meldgen Old Science. The Old Science techniques had been lost ages ago, although an occasional **artefact** still turned up here and there.

'And this is a product of the Old Science?' Gregor asked.

'Right. It's a Meldgen Free Producer. I doubt if there are more than four or five of them in the entire universe. They're **unduplicatable**.'

'What does it produce?' Gregor asked.

'How should I know?' Arnold said. 'Hand me the Meldge–English dictionary, will you?'

---

periphery: outer or surrounding area
artefact: something made by (human) art and workmanship
unduplicatable: impossible to copy

Keeping a stern rein on his patience, Gregor walked to the bookshelf. 'You don't know what it produces –'

'Dictionary. Thank you. What does it matter what it produces? It's *free*! This machine grabs energy out of the air, out of space, the sun, anywhere. You don't have to plug it in, fuel or service. It runs indefinitely.'

Arnold opened the dictionary and started to look up the words on the front of the Producer.

'Free energy –'

'Those scientists were no fools,' Arnold said, jotting down his translation on a pocket pad. 'The Producer just grabs energy out of the air. So it really doesn't matter what it turns out. We can always sell it, and anything we get will be pure profit.'

Gregor stared at his dapper little partner, and his long, unhappy face became sadder than ever.

'Arnold,' he said, 'I'd like to remind you of something. First of all, you are a chemist. I am an ecologist. We know nothing about machinery and less than nothing about complicated alien machinery.'

Arnold nodded absently and turned a dial. The Producer gave a dry gurgle.

'What's more,' Gregor said, retreating a few steps, 'we are planetary **decontaminationists**. Remember? We have no reason to –'

The Producer began to cough unevenly.

'Got it now,' Arnold said. 'It says, "The Meldge Free Producer, another triumph of Glotten Laboratories. This Producer is Warranted Indestructible, Unbreakable, and Free of All Defects. No Power Hook-up Is Required. To Start, Press Button One. To Stop, Use Laxian Key. Your Meldge Free Producer Comes With an Eternal Guarantee against Malfunction. If Defective in any Way, Please Return at Once to Glotten Laboratories."'

---

decontaminationist: someone responsible for removing pollution

'Perhaps I didn't make myself clear,' Gregor said. 'We are planetary –'

'Don't be stodgy,' Arnold said. 'Once we get this thing working, we can retire. Here's Button One.'

The machine began to clank ominously, then shifted to a steady purr. For long minutes, nothing happened.

'Needs warming up,' Arnold said anxiously.

Then, out of an opening at the base of the machine, a grey powder began to pour.

'Probably a waste product,' Gregor muttered. But the powder continued to stream over the floor for fifteen minutes.

'Success!' Arnold shouted.

'What is it?' Gregor asked.

'I haven't the faintest idea. I'll have to run some tests.'

Grinning triumphantly, Arnold scooped some powder into a test tube and hurried over to his desk.

Gregor stood in front of the Producer, watching the grey powder stream out. Finally he said, 'Shouldn't we turn it off until we find out what it is?'

'Of course not,' Arnold said. 'Whatever it is, it must be worth money.' He lighted his bunsen burner, filled a test tube with distilled water, and went to work.

Gregor shrugged his shoulders. He was used to Arnold's harebrained schemes. Ever since they had formed AAA Ace, Arnold had been looking for a quick road to wealth. His short cuts usually resulted in more work than plain old-fashioned labour, but Arnold was quick to forget that.

Well, Gregor thought, at least it kept things lively. He sat down at his desk and dealt out a complex solitaire.

There was silence in the office for the next few hours. Arnold worked steadily, adding chemicals, pouring off precipitates, checking the results in several large books he kept on his desk. Gregor brought in sandwiches and coffee. After eating, he paced up and down and watched the grey powder tumble steadily out of the machine.

The purr of the Producer grew steadily louder, and the powder flowed in a thick stream.

An hour after lunch Arnold stood up. 'We are in!' he stated.

'What is that stuff?' Gregor asked, wondering if, for once, Arnold had hit upon something.

'That stuff,' Arnold said, 'is Tangreese.' He looked expectantly at Gregor.

'Tangreese, eh?'

'Absolutely.'

'Then would you kindly tell me what Tangreese is?' Gregor shouted.

'I thought you knew. Tangreese is the basic food of the Meldgen people. An adult Meldgen consumes several tons a year.'

'Food, eh?' Gregor looked at the thick grey powder with new respect. A machine which turned out food steadily, 24 hours a day, might be a very good money-maker. Especially if the machine never needed servicing, and cost nothing to run.

Arnold already had the telephone book open. 'Here we are.' He dialled a number. 'Hello, Interstellar Food Corporation? Let me speak to the president. What? He isn't? The vice-president, then. This is important . . . Channels, eh? All right, here's the story. I am in a position to supply you with an almost unlimited quantity of Tangreese, the basic food of the Meldgen people. That's right. I knew you'd be interested. Yes, of course I'll hold on.'

He turned to Gregor. 'These corporations think they can push – yes? . . . Yes sir, that's right, sir. You *do* handle Tangreese, eh? . . . Fine, splendid!'

Gregor moved closer, trying to hear what was being said on the other end. Arnold pushed him away.

'Price? Well, what is the fair market price? . . . Oh. Well, five dollars a ton isn't much, but I suppose – what?

Five *cents* a ton? You're kidding! Let's be serious now.'

Gregor walked away from the telephone and sank wearily into a chair. Apathetically he listened to Arnold saying, 'Yes, yes. Well I didn't know that . . . I see. Thank you.'

Arnold hung up. 'It seems,' he said, 'there's not much demand for Tangreese on Earth. There are only about fifty Meldgens here, and the cost of transporting it to the northern periphery is **prohibitively** high.'

Gregor raised both eyebrows and looked at the Producer. Apparently it had hit its stride, for Tangreese was pouring out like water from a high-pressure hose. There was grey powder over everything in the room. It was half a foot deep in front of the machine.

'Never mind,' Arnold said. 'It must be used for something else.' He returned to his desk and opened several more large books.

'Shouldn't we turn it off in the meantime?' Gregor asked.

'Certainly not,' Arnold said. 'It's *free*, don't you understand? It's making money for us.'

He plunged into his books. Gregor began to pace the floor, but found it difficult wading through the ankle-deep Tangreese. He slumped into his chair, wondering why he hadn't gone into landscape gardening.

By early evening, a grey dust filled the room to a depth of several feet. Several pens, pencils, a briefcase and a small filing cabinet were already lost in it, and Gregor was beginning to wonder if the floor would hold the weight. He had to shovel a path to the door, using a wastepaper basket as an improvised spade.

Arnold finally closed his books with a look of weary satisfaction. 'There *is* another use.'

---

prohibitively: tending to make impossible

'What?'

'Tangreese is used as a building material. After a few weeks' exposure to the air, it hardens like granite, you know.'

'No, I didn't.'

'Get a construction company on the telephone. We'll take care of this right now.'

Gregor called the Toledo-Mars Construction Company and told a Mr O'Toole that they were prepared to supply them with an almost unlimited quantity of Tangreese.

'Tangreese, eh?' O'Toole said. 'Not too popular as a building material these days. Doesn't hold paint, you know.'

'No, I didn't,' Gregor said.

'Fact. Tell you what. Tangreese can be eaten by some crazy race. Why don't you –'

'We prefer to sell it as a building material,' Gregor said.

'Well, I suppose we can buy it. Always some cheap construction going on. Give you fifteen a ton for it.'

'Dollars?'

'Cents.'

'I'll let you know,' Gregor said.

His partner nodded sagely when he heard the offer. 'That's all right. Say this machine of ours produces ten tons a day, every day, year after year. Let's see . . .' He did some quick figuring with his slide rule. 'That's almost five hundred and fifty dollars a year. Won't make us rich, but it'll help pay the rent.'

'But we can't leave it here,' Gregor said, looking with alarm at the ever-increasing pile of Tangreese.

'Of course not. We'll find a vacant lot in the country and turn it loose. They can haul the stuff away any time they like.'

Gregor called O'Toole and said they would be happy to do business.

'All right,' O'Toole said. 'You know where our plant is. Just truck the stuff in any old time.'

'Us truck it in? I thought you –'

'At fifteen cents a ton? No, we're doing you a favour just taking it off your hands. *You* truck it in.'

'That's bad,' Arnold said, after Gregor had hung up. 'The cost of transporting it –'

'Would be far more than fifteen cents a ton,' Gregor said. 'You'd better shut that thing off until we decide what to do.'

Arnold waded up to the Producer. 'Let me see,' he said. 'To turn it off I use the Laxian Key.' He studied the front of the machine.

'Go ahead, turn it off,' Gregor said.

'Just a moment.'

'Are you going to turn it off or not?'

Arnold straightened up and gave an embarrassed little laugh. 'It's not that easy.'

'Why not?'

'We need a Laxian Key to turn it off. And we don't seem to have one.'

The next few hours were spent in frantic telephone calls around the country. Gregor and Arnold contacted museums, research institutions, the archaeological departments of colleges, and anyone else they could think of. No one had ever seen a Laxian Key or heard of one being found.

In desperation, Arnold called Joe, the Interstellar Junkman, at his downtown penthouse.

'No, I ain't got no Laxian Key,' Joe said. 'Why you think I sold you the gadget so cheap?'

They put down the telephone and stared at each other. The Meldgen Free Producer was cheerfully blasting out its stream of worthless powder. Two chairs and a radiator had disappeared into it, and the grey Tangreese was approaching desktop level.

'Nice little wage earner,' Gregor said.

'We'll think of something.'

'We?'

Arnold returned to his books and spent the rest of the night searching for another use for Tangreese. Gregor had to shovel the grey powder into the hall, to keep their office from becoming completely submerged.

The morning came, and the sun gleamed gaily on their windows through a film of grey dust. Arnold stood up and yawned.

'No luck?' Gregor asked.

'I'm afraid not.'

Gregor waded out for coffee. When he returned, the building superintendent and two large red-faced policemen were shouting at Arnold.

'You gotta get every bit of that sand outa my hall!' the super screamed.

'Yes, and there's an ordinance against operating a factory in a business district,' one of the red-faced policemen said.

'This isn't a factory,' Gregor explained. 'This is a Meldgen Free –'

'I say it's a factory,' the policeman said. 'And I say you gotta cease operation at once.'

'That's our problem,' Arnold said. 'We can't seem to turn it off.'

'Can't turn it off?' The policeman glared at them suspiciously. 'You trying to kid me? I say you *gotta* turn it off.'

'Officer, I swear to you –'

'Listen, wise guy, I'll be back in an hour. You get that thing turned off and this mess out of here, or I'm giving you a summons.' The three men marched out.

Gregor and Arnold looked at each other, then at the Free Producer. The Tangreese was at desktop level now, and coming steadily.

'Damn it all,' Arnold said, with a touch of hysteria, 'there *must* be a way of working it out. There must be a market! It's free. I tell you. Every bit of this powder is free, free, free!'

'Steady,' Gregor said, wearily scratching sand out of his hair.

'Don't you understand? When you get something free, in unlimited quantities, there has to be an application for it. And all this is free –'

The door opened, and a tall, thin man in a dark business suit walked in, holding a complex little gadget in his hand.

'So *here* it is,' the man said.

Gregor was struck by a sudden wild thought. 'Is that a Laxian Key?' he asked.

'A what key? No, I don't suppose it is,' the man said. 'It is a drainometer.'

'Oh,' Gregor said.

'And it seems to have brought me to the source of the trouble,' the man said. 'I'm Mr Garstairs.' He cleared sand from Gregor's desk, took a last reading on his drainometer and started to fill out a printed form.

'What's all this about?' Arnold asked.

'I'm from the Metropolitan Power Company,' Garstairs said. 'Starting around noon yesterday, we observed a sudden enormous drain on our facilities.'

'And it's coming from here?' Gregor asked.

'From that machine of yours,' Garstairs said. He completed his form, folded it and put it in his pocket. 'Thanks for your co-operation. You will be billed for this, of course.' With some difficulty he opened the door, then turned and took another look at the Free Producer.

'It must be making something extremely valuable,' he said, 'to justify the expenditure of so much power. What is it? Platinum dust?'

He smiled, nodded pleasantly and left.

Gregor turned to Arnold. 'Free power, eh?'

'Well,' Arnold said, 'I guess it just grabs it from the nearest power source.'

'So I see. Draws power out of the air, out of space, out of the sun. And out of the power company's lines, if they're handy.'

'So it seems. But the basic principle –'

'To hell with the basic principle!' Gregor shouted. 'We can't turn this damned thing off without a Laxian Key, no one's got a Laxian Key, we're submerged in worthless dust which we can't even afford to truck out, and we're probably burning up power like a sun gone **nova**!'

'There must be a solution,' Arnold said sullenly.

'Yeah? Suppose you find it.'

Arnold sat down where his desk had been and covered his eyes. There was a loud knock on the door, and angry voices outside.

'Lock the door,' Arnold said.

Gregor locked it. Arnold thought for a few moments longer, then stood up.

'All is not lost,' he said. 'Our fortunes will still be made from this machine.'

'Let's just destroy it,' Gregor said. 'Drop it in an ocean or something.'

'No! I've got it now! Come on, let's get the spaceship warmed up.'

The next few days were hectic ones for AAA Ace. They had to hire men, at exorbitant rates, to clear the building of Tangreese. Then came the problem of getting the machine, still spouting grey dust, into their spaceship. But at last, everything was done. The Free Producer sat in the hold, rapidly filling it with Tangreese, and their ship was out of the system and moving fast on overdrive.

'It's only logical,' Arnold explained later. 'Naturally there's no market for Tangreese on Earth. Therefore

---

nova: a star which shows a sudden increase in brightness before dying down

there's no use trying to sell it on Earth. But on the planet Meldge –'

'I don't like it,' Gregor said.

'It can't fail. It costs too much to transport Tangreese to Meldge. But we're moving our entire factory there. We can pour out a constant stream of the stuff.'

'Suppose the market is low?' Gregor asked.

'How low can it get? This stuff is like bread to the Meldgens. It's their basic diet. How can we miss?'

After two weeks in space, Meldge **hove** in sight on their starboard bow. It came none too soon. Tangreese had completely filled the hold. They had sealed it off, but the increasing pressure threatened to burst the sides of the ship. They had to dump tons of it every day, but dumping took time, and there was a loss of heat and air in the process.

So they spiralled into Meldge with every inch of their ship crammed with Tangreese, low on oxygen and extremely cold.

As soon as they had landed, a large orange-skinned customs official came on board.

'Welcome,' he said. 'Seldom do visitors come to our unimportant little planet. Do you expect to stay long?'

'Probably,' Arnold said. 'We're going to set up a business.'

'Excellent!' the official said, smiling happily. 'Our planet needs new blood, new enterprise. Might I inquire what business?'

'We're going to sell Tangreese, the basic food of –'

The official's face darkened. 'You're going to sell what?'

'Tangreese. We have a Free Producer, and –'

The official pressed a button on a wrist dial. 'I am sorry, you must leave at once.'

'But we've got passports, clearance papers –'

---

hove: came

'And we have laws. You must blast off immediately and take your Free Producer with you.'

'Now look here,' Gregor said, 'there's supposed to be free enterprise on this planet.'

'Not in the production of Tangreese there isn't.'

Outside, a dozen army tanks rumbled on to the landing field and ringed themselves around the ship. The official backed out of the port and started down the ladder.

'Wait!' Gregor cried in desperation. 'I suppose you're afraid of unfair competition. Well, take the Free Producer as our gift.'

'No!' Arnold shouted.

'Yes! Just dig it out and take it. Feed your poor with it. Just raise a statue to us some time.'

A second row of army tanks appeared. Overhead, antiquated jet planes dipped low over the field.

'Get off this planet!' the official shouted. 'Do you really think you can sell Tangreese on Meldge? Look around!'

They looked. The landing field was grey and powdery, and the buildings were the same unpainted grey. Beyond them stretched dull grey fields, to a range of low grey mountains.

On all sides, as far as they could see, everything was Tangreese grey.

'Do you mean,' Gregor asked, 'that the whole planet –'

'Figure it out for yourself,' the official said, backing down the ladder. 'The Old Science originated here, and there are always fools who have to tamper with its artefacts. Now get going. But if you ever find a Laxian Key, come back and name your price.'

Age of Retirement
Hal Lynch

In the Golden Age of science fiction, and long before *Star Wars*, there was plenty of high-octane fiction (usually known as 'space-opera') about battles among the stars deciding the fate of galactic empires. In this story, Hal Lynch seems to be suggesting that all this swashbuckling in space is – well – just a bit childish . . .

Eighty miles below us was the south continent of the planet Uriel. I gave the order, and we roared down, down towards the city of Sathos that had never known night,

where the light of four moons filled the sky when the sun was gone. The *Spacebolt* swooped lower over the city, and we dropped our blackness bombs. An inky cloud rose out of Sathos behind us as we arced to return.

I looked across at my troopers, waiting beside the belly-hatch. 'The word is that the city's cleaned out, except for the flickos, and you know just where they'll be hiding. When you hit the streets, blast anything that moves!' Sergeant Kregg grinned, and signalled his boys to switch on their null-gravs. We were over the city again.

'OK, sergeant, let's go get 'em!' I yelled. I led the drop down through the open hatch and into the blackness of Sathos, where the flicko gang waited. They hadn't expected a blackness bomb, they were scattered and confused, but they still knew how to fight. The stun-guns crackled as my troopers dropped into the streets and started hunting the flickos down. Sergeant Kregg and I went after the leaders, who were holed up in their dive downtown. They had a **nauseator** spraying the streets in front of the place, but the sergeant and I managed to keep out of its line of fire while we moved up. We located them on the third floor; it was already getting lighter now.

From behind a set of steps, the sergeant shouted our we're-here-to-help-you summons. They answered with a nauseator blast, but they couldn't reach him. I fired a couple of stun-shots from my side of the street, but they were protected, too.

'Stubborn!' said Kregg. 'You'n' me can pick 'em off, though, soon's it gets light enough.'

'Let's use sleep-gas; I'm in a hurry,' I said. His face filled with disappointment. 'That's an order, sergeant!'

The gas did the job. Soon we had them all 'cuffed and counted'. Kregg called the ship down while I recorded the operation details.

---

nauseator: something that makes people feel sick

'Any injuries, sergeant?'

'One o' them has a skinned elbow; that's all, sir.' He and the troopers herded our prisoners aboard, then he came back.

'Fastest operation I've ever seen,' he said confidentially. 'I'll bet it's a Space Patrol record, sir!'

I knew it was, and felt good about it, but I couldn't let him know it, of course. I just grunted and snapped back his salute. 'Turn 'em over to the local **psychomedics** and bring your troop back to Mars Headquarters. I'm going back with the ship; I'm returning by mattercaster, to make the commander's step-down. Take over, sergeant!'

There were a few old folks at the mattercaster station, but they stepped aside for my blue-and-gold uniform.

'Right in here, captain!' said the attendant, leading me to the nearest booth. I felt a twinge of regret as I settled myself on the cushions. I'd have preferred to have flown my ship back. The *Spacebolt* was certainly the trimmest, fastest ship in the whole sector, and it would have been fitting to have flown her in, but we'd run out of time. Even travelling by mattercaster I'd be lucky to be in time for the ceremony.

When I stepped out of the Patrol receiving booth on Mars I found Wenda waiting for me. She saluted me smartly; prettier than ever in her dress uniform. I realised inwardly that I'd have to watch myself. I'd have to stay away from her if I didn't want to wash myself out a couple of years too early.

'Tommy, I've never been to a Final Review before,' she whispered as we hurried down the corridor. 'Are they very exciting?'

'Almost as dull as travelling by mattercaster.' I didn't mean it, of course. They were wonderful. But I wasn't going to enjoy this one at all.

---

psychomedic: doctor who looks after the minds of the patients

We started down the steps. 'I wonder how the chief's taking it? I mean, knowing this is the last one, and all.'

'I suppose he's got used to the idea,' she said indifferently. We could hear the crowd milling around out on the field now.

Suddenly I just had to tell somebody how I felt. 'It's not fair, Wenda, *it's just not fair!*'

She stopped, and looked at me worriedly. 'You mean making the chief step down? It's for the good of the Patrol, Tommy – you know that. It gives the younger officers a chance.'

'They'll get plenty of chance! Wenda, the chief's as good as he ever was. He can handle anything they throw at him, he –'

'Compulsory retirement at his age is one of the most important Patrol regs! Now, hush – we'll be late!'

As we came out onto the parade ground Colonel Croslake stepped over to meet us. He saluted, and shook my hand.

'Congratulations, Tommy!' he smiled. 'I just heard you stopped another **afflicted** gang!'

'Tommy! You never told me!' said Wenda.

'I picked 'em up on Uriel. It was short and sweet; we were lucky. A little shooting, but no real trouble.'

The colonel clapped me on the shoulder, 'Keep up that sort of work and you'll be staff rank in no time.' *I'd better hurry*, I thought to myself. *The way things are, I'd better hurry!* 'Uh-oh. Guess we'd better fall in. There go the bugles!'

We found our places while the call sounded. Across the parade ground row upon row of pink-cheeked cadets 'snapped to', and stood stiff and silent. In the quiet we could hear the distant noises of the rocket sheds, and the faint stir as the first of the troops marched onto the lower

---

afflicted: suffering; here it is used to describe the 'criminals' (i.e. people who don't fall into line)

end of the field. Then the colour guard appeared, followed by the band, playing the inevitable 'Patrol Alert', and after them the top brass, trim and stern in their new dress blues.

Last of all came the chief, with Halligan, his successor, walking beside him. He already looked older, somehow, and different, though he still marched straight as a ramrod and every inch a soldier. He took his place in the reviewing stand; the band struck up 'The Colours', and the chief watched his troops march past in review for the last time. Picked men they were, from all his old campaigns, here to see the Supreme Commander of the Space Patrol step down. I'm not ashamed to say I felt like crying.

After the last of the troops had passed there was a moment of silence, then the chief made a little speech. I don't remember what he said but it was great. The way he said it made it great. Afterwards he unbuckled his ceremonial belt and fastened it around Commander Halligan's waist while the band struck up 'Honour of The Patrol' and we sang it with tears streaming down our cheeks. Then we cheered until we were hoarse while he went to each one of his staff and shook his hand. While we were cheering I suddenly saw my older brother, Bill, standing in the little crowd of older people at the edge of the field.

Our new CO, Commander Halligan, made a speech, too, but it was sort of an anticlimax. Then we stood Retreat and the chief's Final Review was over. I'd have liked to have had the chance to say something to him personally, but I knew I could never get to him in the crowd. So, as soon as Halligan called 'Dismiss!' I went to find Bill. I avoided Wenda and struggled through the crowd of swarming cadets and troopers to where my brother waited. He grinned down at me.

'Hi, cap'n!' He looked like a stranger in his civvies. We talked for a minute or two about the family – I hadn't seen as much of them recently as I should have – then I led him away from the crowd, down towards the rocket sheds. Things were quieting, and the sun was going down.

'How are things in that, uh . . . philosophy school?' I asked, to be polite.

'Interesting – even exciting, sometimes.'

'I'll bet!'

'I mean it, Tommy. We came across a relationship between music and social thought the other day, that – Well, I'll explain it to you sometime. It's new, and it's wonderful, and it has all kinds of possibilities. By the way, I hear we're going to get your chief, now that he's retired.'

'In your school? You're crazy, Bill!'

'He's got quite a brain, that one. We can use him.'

I stopped walking. 'Listen, Bill, I've got to talk to you,' I said. 'I don't understand this thing. I just don't get it.'

'What's the trouble?'

'Why does the chief have to step down *now*? He's the best we've ever had! Why did they make him quit?'

'If by "they" you mean outsiders, you're wrong, Tommy. Compulsory retirement is the Patrol's own regulation. It wasn't forced on them from outside. Members of the Patrol staff set the age limit themselves. And, of course, it's been set for everybody; the chief's rank doesn't make any difference. He had to step down just as I had to when I reached his age. We just aren't any good any more, kid.'

I grabbed his arm. 'Don't give me that! Before I took my last duty-tour I spent some time up in the library. I was looking through some old visobooks, and I found some stories of the Patrol . . . of the Patrol of a hundred years ago. They had troopers as old as 30, then!'

'Sure, kid, I know. And you may not know it, but if you check on law-forces that go back before the Patrol you'll find they used to have even older men. They recruited at an older age, too. But by the time the Patrol came along it had been found that older men just didn't have the speed of reaction, or the co-ordination to keep up the pace. So they started retiring men younger, and recruiting men younger.

'Then there was another factor: much less killing. Murderers are rarer than Mars clouds these days, but I guess you noticed in those stories that most of the criminals used deadly weapons. In these days of stun-guns and sleep-gas, bringing in the troublemakers is a lot less dangerous. That's helped to lower the recruiting age, and in turn, the retirement age.'

'What're criminals?'

'It's an old word for afflicteds. You never paid enough attention to history, Tommy. You'll have to specialise in it after you step down.'

'I don't even want to think about stepping down,' I growled. 'I've still got two more years. Maybe . . . maybe if I ever get on the staff, I'll be able to change that retirement reg!'

Bill seemed to find that amusing. 'Not a chance, Tommy. They've tried, and it just doesn't work out any other way. When you reach sixteen, Final Review and out you go – for the good of the service!'

'Are you trying to tell me my co-ordination will be shot at sixteen?'

'Look at me,' he grinned. 'At nineteen I'm finished.' Then he got serious. 'No, kid, it isn't that. Something else is missing – a certain spirit, or idealism, or maybe a kind of instinct. You see, our race has changed in the last couple of centuries, Tommy. For one thing, our educational system's been put into high gear, we take on responsibilities sooner than our great-grandfathers did, and by the same token we . . . uh, we settle down a little sooner. Our expansion into space has brought us into contact with dozens of other cultures, some of them centuries older and wiser than ours. So, somehow, we've settled down, as a people, to a different outlook on life than our ancestors had.'

It seemed to me he was getting way off the subject, but I let him talk. We turned and started back towards the parade ground; the sun had set and it was getting pretty dark.

'Tommy, we've started on the big adventure,' he went on. 'We've started on the biggest exploration of all, the exploration of ourselves. That's become so important to us that we don't have time, or inclination, for other things.

'But there are still afflicteds, and I guess there always will be no matter how much the world changes. Somebody's got to take the time and the trouble and the thought to round 'em up and bring 'em in for treatment. Somebody who still has the patience to take authority and routine without sinking into corruption, who can think without brooding and act without anxiety over consequences. Somebody who can fight without hate and live without sorrow, somebody who can give his whole heart to a cause that gives him little or nothing in return.

'So we've turned the job over to you, the younger generation. We've given you the weapons and the know-how, and you've supplied the – heart.'

'Bill, I don't understand a word of what you're talking about. I don't get it.'

'You will, Tommy, you will,' he said quietly in the darkness. 'In a few years you'll see what I mean. The Patrol's found out that after your fifteenth year you somehow "put away these things". The glory dies away, as new yearnings come, until you find yourself a stranger to what you used to be. So the Patrol makes you step down before you reach that point, Tommy. Compulsory retirement, before you stop caring, any more.'

'*Stop caring about the Patrol*? That's crazy!'

'Trouble is, Tommy, you don't care when you're grown up.'

The Top Fifty Things I'd Do If I Ever Became An Evil Overlord

Peter Anspach

Have you ever noticed how, in spite of having better weapons, and being smarter, more powerful and more ruthless than anyone else, the baddy (whether it be Ming The Merciless, Davros or Darth Vader) always gets his come-uppance because of some simple mistake that allows some feeble goody to get the drop on him?

Peter Anspach has. His website, www.eviloverlord.com, has more tips on what not to do if you ever find yourself the hated tyrant of half the galaxy.

Being an Evil Overlord seems to be a good career choice. It pays well, there are all sorts of perks and you can set your own hours. However, every Evil Overlord I've read about in books or seen in movies invariably gets overthrown and destroyed in the end. I've noticed that, no matter whether they are barbarian lords, deranged wizards, mad scientists or alien invaders, they always seem to make the same basic mistakes every single time. With that in mind, allow me to present:

The top fifty things I'd do if I ever became an Evil Overlord

1   My Legions of Terror will have helmets with clear plexiglass visors, not face-concealing ones.
2   My ventilation ducts will be too small to crawl through.
3   My noble half-brother, whose throne I usurped, will be killed, not kept anonymously imprisoned in a forgotten cell of my dungeon.

4 Shooting is *not* too good for my enemies.

5 The artefact which is the source of my power will not be kept on the Mountain of Despair beyond the River of Fire guarded by the Dragons of Eternity. It will be in my safe-deposit box. (The same applies to the object that is my one weakness.)

6 I will not gloat over my enemies' predicament before killing them.

7 When I've captured my adversary and he says, 'Look, before you kill me, will you at least tell me what this is all about?' I'll say, 'No,' and shoot him. No, on second thoughts, I'll shoot him and then say 'No.'

8 I will not include a self-destruct mechanism unless absolutely necessary. If it is necessary, it will not be a big red button labelled 'DANGER: DO NOT PUSH'. The big red button marked 'DO NOT PUSH' will instead trigger a spray of bullets on anyone stupid enough to disregard it. Similarly, the ON/OFF switch will not be clearly labelled as such.

9 All slain enemies will be cremated, or at least have several rounds of ammunition emptied into them – not left for dead at the bottom of the cliff.

10 The hero is not entitled to a last kiss, a last cigarette, or any other last request.

11 I will never employ any device with a digital countdown. If I find that such a device is absolutely unavoidable, I will set it to activate when the counter reaches 117 and the hero is just putting his plan into operation.

12 I will never utter the sentence, 'Before I kill you, there's just one thing I want to know.'

13 When I employ people as advisers, I will occasionally listen to their advice. One of my advisers will be an average five-year-old child. Any flaws in my plan that he is able to spot will be corrected before implementation.

14 Despite its proven stress-relieving effect, I will not indulge in maniacal laughter. When so occupied, it's too easy to miss unexpected developments that a more attentive individual could adjust to accordingly.

15 I will hire a talented fashion designer to create original uniforms for my Legions of Terror, as opposed to some cheap knock-offs that make them look like Nazi storm troopers, Roman footsoldiers or savage Mongol hordes. All were eventually defeated and I want my troops to have a more positive mindset.

16 I will keep a special cache of low-tech weapons and train my troops in their use. That way, even if the heroes manage to neutralise my power generator or render the standard-issue energy weapons useless, my troops will not be overrun by a handful of savages armed with spears and rocks.

17 No matter how well it would perform, I will never construct any sort of machinery that is completely indestructible, except for one small and virtually inaccessible vulnerable spot.

18 I will never build only one of anything important. All important systems will have redundant control panels and power supplies. For the same reason I will always carry at least two fully loaded weapons at all times.

19 My pet monster will be kept in a secure cage from which it cannot escape and into which I could not accidentally stumble.

20 I will dress in bright and cheery colours and so throw my enemies into confusion.

21 All bumbling conjurers, clumsy squires, talentless bards and cowardly thieves in the land will be pre-emptively put to death. My foes will surely give up and abandon their quest if they have no source of comic relief.

22 I will not fly into a rage and kill a messenger who brings me bad news just to illustrate how evil I really am. Good messengers are hard to come by.

23 I will not turn into a snake. It never helps.

24 If I absolutely must ride into battle, I will certainly not ride at the forefront of my Legions of Terror, nor will I seek out my opposite number among his army.

25 When I capture the hero, I will make sure I also get his dog, monkey, ferret or whatever sickeningly cute little animal capable of untying ropes and filching keys happens to follow him around.

26 If I learn the whereabouts of the one artefact that can destroy me, I will not send all my troops out to seize it. Instead I will send them out to seize something else and quietly put a Want-Ad in the local paper.

27 I will hire a team of board-certified architects and surveyors to examine my castle and inform me of any secret passages and abandoned tunnels that I might not know about.

28 If the beautiful princess that I capture says, 'I'll never marry you! Never, do you hear me, NEVER!!!' I will say, 'Oh well' and kill her.

29 My Legions of Terror will be trained in basic marksmanship. Any who cannot hit a man-sized target at ten metres will be used for target practice.

30 Before employing any captured artefacts or machinery, I will carefully read the owner's manual.

31 If it becomes necessary to escape, I will never stop to pose dramatically and toss off a one-liner.

32 I will never build a sentient computer smarter than I am.

33 I will see a competent psychiatrist and get cured of all extremely unusual phobias and bizarre compulsive habits that could prove to be a disadvantage.

34 When my guards split up to search for intruders, they will always travel in groups of at least two. They will be trained so that if one of them disappears mysteriously while on patrol, the other will immediately initiate an alert and call for back-up instead of quizzically peering round a corner.

35 I will instruct my Legions of Terror to attack the hero en masse instead of standing around waiting while members break off and attack him one or two at a time.

36 If the hero runs up to my roof, I will not run up after him and struggle with him in an attempt to push him over the edge. I will also not engage him at the edge of a cliff. (In the middle of a rope-bridge over a river of molten lava is not even worth considering.)

37 If I am fighting with the hero atop a moving platform, have disarmed him and am about to finish him off, and he glances behind me and drops flat, I too will drop flat instead of quizzically turning round to find out what he saw.

38 I will not shoot at any of my enemies if they are standing in front of the crucial support beam to a heavy, dangerous, unbalanced structure.

39 If I'm eating dinner with the hero, put poison in his goblet, then have to leave the table for any reason, I will order new drinks for both of us instead of trying to decide whether or not to switch with him.

40 I will not have captives of one sex guarded by members of the opposite sex.

41 I will not use any plan in which the final step is horribly complicated, e.g. 'Align the twelve stones of power on the sacred altar then activate the medallion at the moment of total eclipse.' Instead it will be more along the lines of 'Push the button.'

42 My vats of hazardous chemicals will be covered when not in use. Also, I will not construct walkways above them.

43 If a group of henchmen fail miserably at a task, I will not berate them for incompetence and then send the same group out to try the task again.

44 I will not design my Main Control Room so that every workstation is facing away from the door.

45 If I decide to hold a double execution of the hero and an underling who failed or betrayed me, I will see to it that the hero is scheduled to go first.

46 When arresting prisoners, my guards will not allow them to stop and grab a useless trinket of purely sentimental value.

47 My dungeon will have its own qualified medical staff complete with bodyguards so that if a prisoner becomes sick and his cellmate tells the guard it's an emergency, the guard will fetch a trauma team instead of opening up the cell for a look.

48 My dungeon cells will not be furnished with objects that contain reflective surfaces or anything that can be unravelled.

49 Any data file of crucial importance will be padded to 1.45MB in size.

50 Finally, to keep my subjects permanently locked in a mindless trance, I will provide each of them with free unlimited Internet access.

Heinemann
New Windmills

Founding Editors: Anne and Ian Serraillier

Chinua Achebe Things Fall Apart
David Almond Skellig
Maya Angelou I Know Why the Caged Bird Sings
Margaret Atwood The Handmaid's Tale
Jane Austen Pride and Prejudice
J G Ballard Empire of the Sun
Stan Barstow Joby; A Kind of Loving
Nina Bawden Carrie's War; Devil by the Sea; Kept in the Dark; The
Finding; Humbug
Lesley Beake A Cageful of Butterflies
Malorie Blackman Tell Me No Lies; Words Last Forever
Ray Bradbury The Golden Apples of the Sun; The Illustrated Man
Betsy Byars The Midnight Fox; The Pinballs; The Not-Just-Anybody
Family; The Eighteenth Emergency
Victor Canning The Runaways
Jane Leslie Conly Racso and the Rats of NIMH
Susan Cooper King of Shadows
Robert Cormier We All Fall Down; Heroes
Roald Dahl Danny, The Champion of the World; The Wonderful
Story of Henry Sugar; George's Marvellous Medicine; The BFG;
The Witches; Boy; Going Solo; Matilda; My Year
Anita Desai The Village by the Sea
Charles Dickens A Christmas Carol; Great Expectations;
Hard Times; Oliver Twist; A Charles Dickens Selection
Berlie Doherty Granny was a Buffer Girl; Street Child
Roddy Doyle Paddy Clarke Ha Ha Ha
Anne Fine The Granny Project
Jamila Gavin The Wheel of Surya
Graham Greene The Third Man and The Fallen Idol; Brighton Rock
Thomas Hardy The Withered Arm and Other Wessex Tales
L P Hartley The Go-Between
Ernest Hemmingway The Old Man and the Sea; A Farewell to Arms
Barry Hines A Kestrel For A Knave
Nigel Hinton Getting Free; Buddy; Buddy's Song; Out of the Darkness
Anne Holm I Am David
Janni Howker Badger on the Barge; The Nature of the Beast;
Martin Farrell

Pete Johnson The Protectors
Jennifer Johnston Shadows on Our Skin
Geraldine Kaye Comfort Herself
Daniel Keyes Flowers for Algernon
Dick King-Smith The Sheep-Pig
Elizabeth Laird Red Sky in the Morning; Kiss the Dust
D H Lawrence The Fox and The Virgin and the Gypsy; Selected Tales
George Layton The Swap
Harper Lee To Kill a Mockingbird
C Day Lewis The Otterbury Incident
Joan Lingard Across the Barricades; The File on Fraulein Berg
Penelope Lively The Ghost of Thomas Kempe
Jack London The Call of the Wild; White Fang
Bernard MacLaverty Cal; The Best of Bernard Mac Laverty
James Vance Marshall Walkabout
Ian McEwan The Daydreamer; A Child in Time
Michael Morpurgo My Friend Walter; The Wreck of the Zanzibar;
The War of Jenkins' Ear; Why the Whales Came; Arthur, High King
of Britain; Kensuke's Kingdom; Hereabout Hill
Beverley Naidoo No Turning Back
Bill Naughton The Goalkeeper's Revenge
New Windmill A Charles Dickens Selection
New Windmill Book of Classic Short Stories
New Windmill Book of Fiction and Non-fiction: Taking Off!
New Windmill Book of Haunting Tales
New Windmill Book of Humorous Stories: Don't Make Me Laugh
New Windmill Book of Nineteenth Century Short Stories
New Windmill Book of Non-fiction: Get Real!
New Windmill Book of Non-fiction: Real Lives, Real Times
New Windmill Book of Scottish Short Stories
New Windmill Book of Short Stories: Fast and Curious
New Windmill Book of Short Stories: From Beginning to End
New Windmill Book of Short Stories: Into the Unknown
New Windmill Book of Short Stories: Tales with a Twist
New Windmill Book of Short Stories: Trouble in Two Centuries
New Windmill Book of Short Stories: Ways with Words
New Windmill Book of Short Stories by Women
New Windmill Book of Stories from many Cultures and Traditions:
Fifty-Fifty Tutti-Frutti Chocolate-Chip
New Windmill Book of Stories from Many Genres: Myths, Murders
and Mysteries

How many have you read?